MANNEQUIN

CH'OE YUN

MANNEQUIN
A NOVEL

TRANSLATED BY
JUNG YEWON

DALKEY ARCHIVE PRESS

Originally published in Korean as Maneking by Yolimwon Publishing Group in 2003.

Copyright © 2003 by Ch'oe Yun
Translation copyright © 2016 by Jung Yewon
First Dalkey Archive edition, 2016

Library of Congress Cataloging-in-Publication Data

Names: Ch'oe, Yun, 1953- author. | Jung, Yewon, translator.
Title: Mannequin / Ch'oe Yun ; translated by Jung Yewon.
Other titles: Manek'ing. English
Description: First Dalkey Press edition. | Victoria, TX : Dalkey Archive
    Press, 2016.
Identifiers: LCCN 2016031195 | ISBN 9781628971521 (pbk. : alk. paper)
Subjects: LCSH: Beauty--Fiction. | Women--Korea (South)--Fiction. | Korea
    (South)--Social life and customs--Fiction.
Classification: LCC PL992.18.Y86 M3613 2016 | DDC 895.73/4--dc23
LC record available at https://lccn.loc.gov/2016031195

Partially funded by a grant by the Illinois Arts Council, a state agency
Published in collaboration with the Literature Translation Institute of Korea

Dalkey Archive Press publications are, in part, made possible through the
support of the University of Houston-Victoria and its programs in creative
writing, publishing, and translation.

Dalkey Archive Press
Victoria, TX / McLean, IL / Dublin
www.dalkeyarchive.com

Cover design and composition by Mikhail Iliatov
Printed on permanent/durable acid-free paper

That's how it all began.
As though it were the end, not the beginning.

Table of Contents

Part One

Jini is my family and my universe,
my work, my love, my child.

I know the joy of creation.
Jini is the source of all my joy.

I have never encountered a body with such
expressions, lines, and volume as I've found in
Jini's—a body that brings perfect pleasure.

She Sat in the Wind for a Long, Long Time

THE WINTER WIND blows through. It shifts, strikes, pushes, blasts, and then passes. Nearly two seasons have passed already. Maybe two years, or even twenty.

There's music in the winter wind. Music that was written to be played only once, music that's muted when the wind passes on. She lies on her side, listening to music. She lay down like that one clear day, and has been lying in the same position, listening to the music of the wind and the waves, ever since. Her hands are folded on her chest, and her head rests on a little fabric bag that's soft and fragrant. If you listen carefully, you might hear a whistle come from her lips, a light and cheerful sound that somehow awakens the sadness that lies hidden in all hearts. Perhaps you will. Since that clear day, time has passed her by with indifference.

She arrived here by chance one day and lay down as if for a little nap in a half-moon-shaped recess at the top of a rock face, its entrance flanked by trees that kept bad weather at bay. And she came to love this place. She quietly took in the sky that was spread out before her, the sky far away, and the sky even farther away; the sea that could be seen only during the season when the world of trees could be described as one of straight lines and curves; and the scenery around her that she didn't really need to see. Once in a while, a butterfly or two flew to the top of the rock face and stayed. They would sit on the tip of her nose or the crown of her head, then fly around as if to comfort her, and then disappear as though it had suddenly occurred to them that they were lost. Leaves brushed by her and piled up, sometimes filling up cups in her body such as her armpits and curved waist.

Her face is still . . . pale. If anyone saw her, that's what they would say. But who on earth would see her?

"Just a minute . . . right there . . . that light . . . up there . . . far . . . but near . . ."

Occasionally, people passed by the recess where she lay. Judging from their short breaths, there must have been a very steep trail there. But not everyone was fortunate enough to climb up so high. The wind swallowed the voices that passed beyond, panting and dying away. The wind shifted for a moment, then made its own voice heard, moving sharply from high to low pitches.

Where was this place with light that was far away but seemed near, or was near but seemed far away? This place spoken of by the many voices rambling through. Everyone climbed up the hill, longing for light in the night, in the wind. The people passing by all climbed toward the light above, which seemed far away but was near. At one time, she, too, had climbed toward an unknown place above her. What and who was at that place? She, too, had once longed for it, like those who now climbed the slope. Not anymore. Now, she longs for nothing. She has become part of this place.

The wind, stronger now for the sounds it has swallowed, pushes everything that's drifting in the air up toward her. No one can pause in that wind, and so no one can see her face. She can't see anyone wandering through, either. There is no one she wants to see. There is, in the end, no one she needs to see, no one she needs to leave.

Was there no one she longed for? No one she loved?

None can speak for her. The face of the woman sitting in the cold wind wears an expression that brings nothing specific to mind. Or perhaps you could say that the face can bring almost anything to mind.

There must have been someone she missed. There must have been someone she wanted to walk barefoot with on the sand, arms linked together, just before the sun rose on the beach, before the world began. She, too, must have longed to be with someone when the grains of sand, swept up in the waves, tickled the soles of her feet as she stood still, taking in the sensation. Perhaps she wanted to be with her parents and siblings, who flocked around her to toss her high up in the air like a light, rubber ball in the noisy schoolyard on a sunny autumn day after a track meet. Perhaps even now they were gathered together, looking worried, as if she'd been tossed up into the air and disappeared into the clouds on that day long ago, mumbling, "Yes, she was a promising little girl, my daughter, my sister . . ."

But nothing like that had ever happened. Things like that took place only in her imagination. She watched such scenes from up close and far away, longing for them to happen to her. She, too, could have wished for such simple joy once. Before she came too far, when things were very simple.

But not all wishes are fulfilled. It isn't that hard, however, to put such petty desires to rest, and finally, to forget. People say at times that trivial desires have a greater hold on the soul. Perhaps that's true. Perhaps that's why many people leave somewhere only to return there for the same reason.

In winter, the pitch of the wind becomes more refined. Spring or summer could never match it. There are summer storms, of course. But could storms be considered wind? Just as the sea has dozens of names on an island nation in the Pacific, the sound of wind that she can hear in this place must have hundreds, thousands of names. No wind is the same as the wind that's just passed, or the wind that's to follow. Just like the sea. A consistent wind could have a name, but perhaps a consistent wind is no wind at all. Just as a steady current is not a current.

She is lying here so that she may have both the wind and the sea. Neither the wind nor the sea can possess her. She no longer belongs to anyone.

The good thing is that the wind comes blowing day and night. The wind never rests. The wind has never stopped. It's a rare moment when the wind doesn't cause thin blades of grass to stir. Even in those moments, she knows, the wind stirs elsewhere. It's like the sea, which is never entirely still.

The wind is always moving, and the movement is more unpredictable than any other movement in the world. How can she stop hoping when such movement exists? From time to time the wind dries her cheeks, where one or two teardrops remain, ruffles up her hair, taps on her stiffened face as if on a xylophone, then carves a smile on the face, and finally, helps her move from a solid world to one that's in flux, from form to abstraction, from chromatic colors to achromatic, and at last, helps her move far away from the world.

There's no longer anyone climbing up the steep path toward the place up above. It's deep in the night. She sees the swollen bulk of the world sinking into the shadow of darkness. At last, it's time for her to rest.

Pink Anemone

THAT'S HOW EVERYTHING began. As if it were the end, not the beginning.

My prolonged drifting is finally coming to an end, and a life of stability is about to start. The moment I thought that, I saw the most dazzling thing in the world and my life was upended in an instant. My goals in life became mixed up in that moment, and never returned to their proper place. Their place? What place? It would be more precise to say that I lost sight of my goals in an instant.

The things I had wanted so desperately to achieve became tedious and boring. I would stop and sigh every few steps while walking up hill on my way to work, the hill I used to walk up every day humming, and for the first time I smelled something repulsive in the petunias in full bloom in the flower garden. I was too young to end everything and too old to start over.

But whenever I think of what I saw that day, I feel an intense joy, almost as intense as what I felt that day, course through my body. The same thrill I feel when I sense the water pressure on my skin after I jump, fully equipped in my diving suit, from a yacht's deck deep into the sea. Yes. It happened so naturally in the sea, like fate.

That day, we regrouped around fifteen meters underwater. The diving journey, planned in celebration of my marriage with D, was undertaken mostly by our close friends. A Japanese woman who happened to come on the journey with us, as well as a middle-aged man who was a lifer in the Navy, willingly joined in. Aside from those two, everyone had come diving with us at least three times. We entered the water after traveling from the forest island for about seven minutes on the boat.

It was kind of a night-before-the-wedding party thrown by the sea, with ideal conditions that would go down in history, with amazing views and visibility. A different world, swaying in primary colors beyond description, was spread out on the seabed made up of rocks and gravel. It was only in a sea like that that my mind could rest peacefully without interference.

"Not comfort or liberation from something, but absolute peace. Do you want to experience a state where your body seems to become completely immaterial? Then you should learn to appreciate the world under the sea." I would often say this to my friends. Perhaps the fact that I said such things is evidence that I still didn't know much about the world under the sea. It seemed like just yesterday that D, who couldn't even swim, first came to a meeting held by the scuba diving club at work. Soon D navigated the sea like a mermaid or a siren, moving her two fins freely at will.

Looking straight at me, who was in charge of odd-jobs in the club, D said, "Can you join the diving club even if you don't know how to swim at all?"

The pressure gauge indicated that there was still a substantial amount of oxygen, so we had no intention of ascending. Besides, the diving that day was undertaken in our honor.

We had stopped not only for safety depressurization, but also because we wanted to enjoy, just the two of us, the final trance before leaving the water, watching the spectacle under the sea with the yellow coral fields filling up the rock valley, the school of blue-lined angelfish, as well as schools of blackfin sweeper and damselfish that surrounded us as if to caress us. A friend, who had gone diving before his own wedding, had encouraged the journey, saying, 'The scene under the sea the day before the wedding was especially beautiful.' I don't know if it was because of what he said, but it really was spectacular that day under the sea. While the others played with big-headed fish and shrimp that appeared among rocks and then disappeared, we swam around in a feast of brilliant colors, where the water temperature reached about nineteen degrees Celsius. I think they moved over to the rocks so that the two of us could swim around for about five minutes. D turned around to look at me, suspended in the water, moving her hands slowly.

D raised her left hand and pointed to her chest. Then she put her hand on her head. And then she looked around, and stretched her right hand up and her left hand down in a curve. This last motion was one we knew quite well. But it was an exchange we could have only when we were alone underwater.

"Look at me. I like you. I love you."

All unusual movements underwater can be taken as danger signals by other divers. D's last motion, in particular, not to be found in any diver's book, could have been seen that way. The only ones looking at D were the aquatic plants, the fish, and myself. I liked seeing D under the blue sea more than anywhere else. One who has tasted the beauty of the world under the sea cannot resist the dangerous seduction of scuba diving. It was also in such moments under the sea when D and I were most perfectly in sync.

At that moment, a school of brilliant white fish, smaller than anchovies, passed between us as if to respond to D's signal. I waited for the school of fluorescent bodies to disappear, and answered D.

I raised both my hands and brought them together above my head. Then I pulled my right hand toward myself a couple of times. Then I did the last motion, for D alone, raising one hand over my head in a pliant curve, and stretching the other hand out as well in a downward curve.

"I like you too. Come here. I love you."

It was a method of conversing in water that we had come up with one day three years earlier.

Before I finished my motion, one of the other divers signaled that we should ascend, and we began to swim, apace with our bubbles, toward the surface where the blue was lighter. When we sensed that the surface wasn't far from us, the incredible thing happened. At first, I doubted my own eyes. How far down were we? I don't know whether I felt that there was no one around but D and me because everyone else had gone out of the water, or if I just don't remember correctly. Whatever the case, whenever I recall the scene, I see the deserted sea, suddenly empty, the two of us left alone in the vast emptiness. If, at that moment, a blue-lined snapper, startled by a descending object, hadn't drawn a quick, long arc, I would have simply thought that the scene was a hallucination, created by light and a state of excitement.

It was because of a woman, descending from the lightness above, that D and I stopped ascending almost simultaneously. The woman, curled up like a baby in its mother's womb and wearing an almost transparent suit of blue, nearly indistinguishable from the color of the sea, was coming down toward us. With a gentle expression on her face as if resting, with the sea as her bed, she descended with her eyes closed. The thin fabric shrouding her body waved in the current, making her look like a mysterious goddess surrounded by transparent aquatic plants. A little goddess descending toward none other than myself.

There was no stirring in the peaceful expression on her face, an intensely gentle expression that suddenly touched my heart and caused an outpouring of emotion concentrated in the form of tears. Where had I seen such an expression before, an expression that was fit for the moment when the boundary between life and death became obsolete?

D and I stopped moving and looked at the descending body. Whether or not our eyes met in that moment I don't know. No, I think it was the opposite. We must have forgotten each other completely. The woman in the blue suit opened her eyes, kept them open for a moment, and closed them again, when she came near us. As if to say, "I'm here." As if pure air, not water, surrounded her. It was almost dangerous to come that deep down without being fully equipped.

The danger was brief, however. There wasn't any time for me to approach the woman. D must have been thinking the same thing. We began moving in the same direction, then came to a stop. Divers with underwater cameras appeared in an instant, and a little later, D and I were out of the water. I don't remember how I got back on the boat, how and when I put the equipment away, where D was, and how we returned to the forest island. That was all. The next day was our wedding day, so we left for the hotel in Seogwipo where we had a reservation. Only later did I learn, from a conversation among the staff at the hotel coffee shop, that a major company had been filming an ad for a new air conditioner that was to be launched. But I didn't dare ask them for more specific information, with D's strange silence and stiff expression. D's condition that day was different from the peculiar, detached state that came over her from time to time when she came out of the water after a dive.

The entry in my diving log that day is as follows.

Date: 19 September
Location: around Forest Island
Name of partner: Pink Anemone
Time of entry into water: 12:36
Time of exit out of water: 13:11
Time underwater: 35 minutes
Maximum depth of water: 26 meters
Range of visibility: about 12 meters
Water temperature: 19.7°C
Conditions on the sea floor: rocks and gravel

I don't know how, and in what state of mind, I was able to make a record like that. But the log was mine and so was the handwriting, no doubt about it. Thirty-five minutes underwater. About one minute longer than the other peoples' time underwater. The expansive, yet brief moment in which D and I saw the woman underwater was no more than one minute. That one minute became a point of no return in my life and in D's life. Strangely, whenever I take a look at this log, I picture a shoe in my mind—a shoe on the foot of the woman underwater. Along with the other shoe drifting around in the faintly lit underwater world, vast and desolate.

The wedding was held the next day. There was no hesitation or doubt. It was like our last destination. Like a polite hand-shake between athletes after a long, arduous game. The guests consisted of the fish in the sea and our friends who had come to congratulate us on our wedding. The ceremony, held at the tangerine orchard where we had made a reservations was simple. The congratulatory message shared by a friend who officiated, for the reason that he'd just become a pastor, was short. Six months before, D had been persuaded by my words that if it didn't make a difference whether or not we had a wedding, it would be better to have one. I can't say, however, that I put her family's opposition to rest, for no one in her family attended the wedding. Most people who came to the wedding were D's and my mutual friends. From my family came my aunt, who had raised me, and a cousin. I was willing to provide plane tickets for any extended family who would come all the way to Jeju Island; for all of them, if they wanted to come. But I didn't have that many relatives, as my family was originally from North Korea, and it was enough for me that those two had come. My aunt, who I was seeing for the first time in nearly five years, was somewhat excited because it had been her first flight ever.

I can't say that the relationship of four years, which culminated in marriage, had always been smooth. In my mind, romantic relationships lasted because they didn't always go smoothly. Why did people have such relationships, then? Because they enjoyed the ups and downs. I was the same.

If it weren't for the diving club, D and I wouldn't have come this far.

So what in the world had happened?

I think I took a nap until evening, after returning to the hotel. When I opened my eyes, sensing the bleakness penetrating my bones in the dusk, the bride-to-be was gazing at the darkness, her back turned from me and her eyes wide open. She wasn't crying, and she wasn't angry, either.

I had a feeling that she knew. She knew what lay at the heart of the change that I myself couldn't put my finger on. But without saying anything to each other, we celebrated the night before the wedding with our friends, and then went through with the wedding, as planned, the next morning at eleven. The wedding proceeded, suppressing the resistance emerging from elsewhere, the way people jump into the sea even when they see a violent breaker rise. Our friends left, and D and I went to see the water in formal white dress and suit, and with a white car covered in fancy lace decorations.

And that night, D, or Pink Anemone, died at sea.

Starfish

YEAH, I'M SMOKING another cigarette. I jump to my feet and looked at the clock. 4:20 a.m. The night is over. The dawn's breaking. I hear a cough now and then, but the main room is still quiet. It's my mom coughing. In about an hour this house will be in an uproar as usual. It's been that way every day for more than two months now. "We still have no news," the voice on the phone will probably say. Two investigators, Park and Yi, have been given a secret commission to look for Jini. Their answer will always be the same, of course. I have a feeling that for a while, they'll have nothing to say. They can't search every street, every alleyway in the world, the vast sea and the countless mountains.

When the morning phone call has been made, the sighs of the four people living in this house will be heard, and the people, who had gathered in the living room for a moment, will scatter away, each to his or her own room. Their sighs sound different every day, in subtle ways.

There has been no news yet that Jini's name has been found on the list of the unidentified dead. No, not yet.

"Yi Jina, it's Yi Jina!"

Each time, someone in the family shouts urgently at the personnel in charge. I don't know why they think they have to be urgent whenever they're on the phone. When I make a call, I do it quietly.

"Please let me know if there's been any news regarding Yi Jina. I'm her sister, Yi Jeong-a. If you'd like identification, I'll give you my resident registration number."

Calls of this kind are made by me, or Shark, or Conch. Oh, Shark is my brother's nickname. His friends at school began calling him that when he was little, his name being Sangho, which sounds like sang-eo, which means shark, and now, the nickname is used more often than his name. Have you seen a shark? When we were young, we used to take a close look at sharks in an illustrated book of fish. We were bored. The house was always empty, and it was cold outside. And good things to eat, as well as fun things to do, were too far away. The sharks we saw in the illustrated book when we were young were beautiful, violent, and ruthless. Once they sank their teeth into their prey, they never let go. We really liked the way they looked and acted. You don't provoke sharks. You never know when and how they might attack you. They're sharks, after all. In our house, everyone goes by a nickname. Conch is Ms. Kim's nickname. She was given the nickname because her ears look like conches. And my mom's disheveled hair is why we call her Agar-Agar when she's not around.

My mom never makes the phone call to see if Jini's dead or alive. She's busy with other things. She's, what should I say, someone who prays for the peace of all mankind. That's why she climbs mountains so often.

When we were young, she was always out working in someone else's home or in the market, but now, with Jini gone, she's busy doing things like climbing mountains to pray. It's a good thing that Shark and I are no longer so young that we, being in an empty house, ache to do something out of fear or boredom. Things are different now. We like it better without her.

In the end, it was decided that Shark and I would take turns making the calls. I would make the call one day, and Shark the next, and so on. We haven't heard yet if Jini is alive or dead. Conch is against trying to find Jini's name on the list of the unidentified dead, saying that the act may turn Jini's fate in that direction. Sometimes, when Shark shouts Yi Jina into the receiver, the name, which was given to her when she was born seventeen years ago, sounds unfamiliar to me, even though I've called her by that name and heard it being called countless times when I was little. Of course it does. The fact that Jini is called by her real name is an ominous sign that she has disappeared to a corner of the world where the name Jini has no meaning.

Will there be any news of Jini today? To be honest, I'd be just as anxious to hear any news as to hear nothing. What kind of news could there be? There's an equal chance of hearing good news, that she's safe and well somewhere, and hearing the most extremely unfortunate news. So around this time every morning, the family turns to this kind of a solution. Everyone despairs constantly, there being no clue or news, but we have as much hope as we do despair that she hasn't been found dead yet. Like a soap opera showing at the same hour every day, the soap opera of this house shows reruns every morning, each time just a little different. Only afterward can everyone go to his or her own room. You have to show that you care at least that much when someone in the family has disappeared, right?

Shark is quite dejected. It won't last long, though. I trust the blood cells of tedium, rage, and hatred going around in our bodies. They'll make us come alive again. Conch has forgotten what she has to do. Now that Jini is gone, both Shark and Conch are dithering. It's as if they've lost their jobs. That's why Shark gets angry. When he gets angry, he starts beating people and things. When he makes a scene like that, I feel refreshed as well. But I'm different. I found something to do as soon as Jini left home.

Shark has no interest or skill in anything unrelated to Jini. He always says, "I don't want to learn anything." He jokes around, saying, "I'm a Jini specialist." How much Jini gets paid for every minute of an appearance or filming, for the filming of her face and body, of the nape of her neck, which is at the top of wanted lists for ad proposals, and of her hands, feet, elbows, and even her auricles . . . Shark is the only one who knows the price of all the particulars of Jini's body. He's been doing only this work for many years now.

Actually, Shark doesn't have the sharp teeth or the well-developed muscles of the sharks in the illustrated book of fish. He looks delicate, like a girl, with a pale face and a thin body. But he's tall, toned from rigorous workouts, and rather good-looking. That's our weapon, bait, and asset. It runs in the family. They say that my grandfather and his brothers were all handsome. Fair is fair, they say. Once, Shark and I stole something at the market. Just for practice. We knew we were found out, so we stashed what we stole in the shop next door. But the shop owner just tilted his head and went back to his own shop after seeing us looking up at him, the picture of innocence. Shark was eight, and I was six. We know very well how to fool people. It's a piece of cake. Even now, we'll be walking down the street, and we'll wink at each other and steal something. We don't do it all the time, but we do it for a thrill now and then. We never get caught.

Shark is scary when he gets angry. He turns viciously on his family, like someone off his medicine. Not because we're family. He says he's against those primates called humans. Still, he said a few days ago, "Jini's going to come back on Mom's birthday. So make sure to set the table for a birthday feast!"

For the first time in years, my mom was going to have a feast thrown in her honor. Shark threatened us so we wouldn't start dinner before he came home, but he came home very late at night. We were all starving to death, but we waited without eating. Jini didn't come—there wasn't even a phone call. When it was midnight, Shark kicked the table, knocking it over. My mom didn't even get to touch her own birthday feast when it had been so long since she'd had one. I can't really imagine Jini forgetting my mom's birthday. I've seen Jini cry many times because of my mom. She cried like a wounded animal moaning, because she couldn't talk. Whenever I saw her crying, I thought, "She's beautiful even when she cries." So I would let her cry. That's the way it is—life is no big deal. It's like a gift that comes with a purchase. Some of them you like, but some you just can't stand.

There's a tacit understanding between Shark and me. Sometimes, we meet downtown and go into a hotel. And we take off our worldly shells and comfort each other, lying still with our flesh rubbing against each other. Because we're pitiful. Because we're primates that have stopped evolving. We order expensive room service, and make a toast to Jini, who's made such pleasure possible. If people who knew we were brother and sister saw us, they'd jump to conclusions and point fingers at us. But we're not interested in what people might think. What we want is simply the comfort of our flesh. We can momentarily forget the tedious affairs of the world as we relish in our own soft, resilient flesh. That's the only time when Shark is soft. We become children and fall into a deep, long sleep, side by side.

We meet in this way and do business. I make sure to modify our tacit contract. Shark keeps a record in a little notebook. Through many negotiations, I've increased my share to include Jini's hands, nape, and hair. The income from those parts of Jini's body becomes mine. I've earned quite a sum this way. Saving money without any particular aim, that's my hobby. I don't spend it on anyone, not even myself. Shark says that I'm just one of the many money collectors everywhere.

Shark, of course, has a monopoly on Jini's whole body, feet, face, arms, and so on, which are the most popular with advertisers. At any rate, he's in charge of arranging the contracts, collecting the down payments, increasing revenue, and taking Jini to shoots and interviews. He even supervises the household expenses and Conch's salary. We like transparent, precise dealings. When I open my eyes, Shark is always gone. That's the way it is. We understand each other, but we don't have much to say to each other.

It was one summer day when Jini was three months old that she was discovered by someone from an ad agency. The life of the young couple who'd come to Seoul from a farming village where they worked on someone else's farm began to take a turn for the better because of their youngest daughter. My father was working as a porter at the marketplace, and my mother was selling Chinese cabbages at a corner in the marketplace. I can't picture, for the life of me, Agar-Agar holding a baby, shouting "Take home some Chinese cabbages!" Had she, too, been that passionate at one time? At any rate, the baby was spotted by someone who was looking for a model for an ad. It happened too long ago for me to remember. It's something I've heard. There are only two things I remember: my father's sudden death, and Jini's laughter.

My father died when things got so good that he no longer had to do hard work. I remember his death because of the peculiar excitement that was in the air before he died. And because that's when Jini began to suffer from a speech disorder. I sensed that something had changed. I think I remember my father's death because of the luster and leisure that was suddenly a part of our home, and the furtive effort to keep things hushed. Because even before the excitement passed, he had come down with a disease and passed away. It must have been too much for him. There are people like that, who never get to enjoy anything, and the first chance they get to enjoy something, they up and die. Mom says that he died early because he'd been through such hardship when he was younger, but I don't agree. Not at all. There are a lot of people like that in the world, people who don't know how to accept a gift from the world, people who can't rest easy until they destroy the gift. I think Shark and I take after our father a little in that way, because we, too, hate to enjoy things. What is there to enjoy so much in the world, anyway?

A nice house, that's something you can rent with money. Imagine being cooped up in the same house every day—isn't that horrific? Why do you think we go to hotels?

Nice clothes, those things you don't need to wear twice, like the finest garments Jini puts on only once. When I get bored with clothes, I discard them.

Good food, that's something you can have as much of as you want. Just hang around parties that are held at dozens of places every night. People are easily fooled by makeup. People love counterfeits. Do you know how many people came up to me on the set, taking me for Jini? It's simply because Jini hates wearing makeup when she's not working, and I enjoy wearing makeup and dressing up. If you're good at putting on makeup and dressing up, you can taste all the finest dishes provided at parties held at dozens of places every night. Shark and I love doing stuff like that. We both put on thick makeup and rent the finest dresses and suits from rental shops. Then we sneak into Mr. So-and-So's dinner party, and Miss So-and-So's reception. We enjoy the food and the drinks and the music. The music usually sucks at parties like that, but there are some exceptions. Those are the ones we pick.

Sometimes, stupid people come up to us and we introduce ourselves as experimental artists. We tell them we're visiting from New York. But if they ask anything further, that's it. We shut our mouths, and look straight into their eyes for a long time with haughty stares. We never get stared down. It's easy. You just act as if the person in front of you isn't there. They back away quickly, without exception. As soon as we get home, we throw up everything we ate, drank, and saw. We feel so much better afterward.

Let me talk about Jini's laughter. I don't remember how many times I've talked about it before. Each time I do, I hope my fear fades away, but the old fear always returns as intense as ever.

Ever since Jini was discovered to be a model when she was three months old, she was in great demand and had to go here and there and everywhere in the country, so she was always sick. She suffered from skin diseases, diarrhea, high fever, constipation, eye diseases, as well as each passing epidemic. For a delicate child, the world is as dangerous as a minefield. All the little things that didn't do a thing to Shark and me, careless as we were, turned into something harmful in her body and made her sick. Flowers and grass where thorns or aphids or some unknown bugs might have been hiding, flavored milk or baby food she kept pestering for, snacks or fruits, a shower of sunshine after a bath when she would squirm around naked, a baby swing that swung back and forth, making her laugh, nails or shards of glass, dirt littered with broken pieces of chinaware . . . all these things were dangerous and off-limits for Jini. All the things we heard about Jini until our ears ached became the unsettling background music of our lives. Careful, careful, careful.

What I feared even more than all the diseases she came down with was her laughter, that laughter on her fifth birthday. How could I forget a special day like that? Back then, she was still Yi Jina. After she was picked up to be a baby model, there had been proposals for ads or photos, but there had never been a contract for her to work exclusively for an agency. The entire household bustled with preparation, although it was nothing compared to the subsequent contracts with terms and conditions improving and down payments increasing almost year after year.

But of course, it wasn't because she knew that the first important contract in her life was about to be signed that she laughed. I can always recall several scenes from that bleak day in early spring, as if I have a videotape in my body that can play them back over and over again.

It was the day I entered elementary school, but that wasn't important to anyone. That's why the day is even more unforgettable. Feeling the still cold, March sunlight on my back, I walked slowly on purpose, trudging along, hoping that someone in the family would come after me. I walked down the shabby neighborhood alleyways, passed the bakery, the stationery shop, and the arcade and arrived at school, but no one in my family came to see me off. Not my father, who was still alive at the time, not my mom, not my brother, not anyone. The only thing that followed me faithfully whenever I looked back was my shadow. I'll remember that forever. I'll never forget that.

Back then, the house was still shabby and we still had to worry about what we would eat the next day, so I understand why the whole family was so consumed with the contract. Buying an outfit with bows and beads for Jini to wear that day meant that the family had to cut back on unnecessary spending for a long time. The spending that had to be curtailed for Jini's outfit included expenses for my snacks and entrance into school, my father's cigarettes, my brother's sports cap, and so on. But that was nothing. Soon enough, when someone wanted and took Jini again, we would receive much more money and be able to eat our fill for a long time. We heard the adults saying over and over again that if the contract was clinched, we'd have nothing to worry about for a while.

At that age, I'd learned many things, and understood the meaning of the lone, solitary road to the entrance ceremony and passively adapted to the situation. That's how I am. I was a precocious child. I understand a lot of things. I just do. But there's a difference between understanding and accepting. I wish people were clear on that.

I understood that everyone was concerned only with the contract, because the person signing the contract with Jini would be coming to the shabby house. But I couldn't accept that no one had come with me to my entrance ceremony. After the ceremony, I kicked and dragged a bottle cap I had found on the ground all the way home. My mind was full of questions about whether the contract had been clinched, the contract on which hung my family's future, and about the important responsibility that had been entrusted to me several days before. Duty was duty, after all.

If the contract was signed, filming would begin the next day. It was an ad for baby clothes. I don't know why it was necessary, but Jini had to laugh out loud. I didn't mind that the responsibility to make her laugh had fallen on me, but I couldn't come up with any ideas as to how to make her laugh, no matter how much I thought about it. When she was a baby, she had laughed easily, her mouth like a half moon. But for some time now, it had been difficult to make her laugh. I tickled her, played peek-a-boo with her, bumped heads with her, and tried everything that would ordinarily make her laugh, but Jini kept her mouth clamped, as if she'd gotten wind of what was to come in her future. So I put off getting home, kicking around the crushed metal bottle cap with my foot instead.

My memory cuts off here, and suddenly turns to the scene in which Jini is laughing out loud. It's always that way when I try to recall that part. The film of my memory must have been damaged at that point. I can't remember for the life of me how I made Jini laugh. I remember that I imitated a funny scene I had seen on television, covering my face with the whipped cream on the birthday cake, but that wasn't what made Jini laugh; it was something I did next, but I don't remember what it was. But I have no desire to do it again, none whatsoever. At any rate, Jini began to laugh, with that adorable look on her face. The problem was what happened next. For some reason, Jini didn't stop laughing but laughed until she almost choked, and only stopped when she was blue in the face and was at the point of suffocation, and then passed out. We were just doing a practice run.

That day was a nightmare. The people shooting the ad left in a hurry, having gotten what they wanted. I sat trembling in a corner. My father carried Jini out, and began to run. The whole family followed him to the only hospital in the neighborhood, which was on the main street, far away from the sloping road. I was afraid to stay alone in the house, where the sound of Jini's incessant, scary laughter still reverberated. So I followed my family, last in line. I think that for the first time I wished Jini would just up and die.

Since that day, Jini never laughed. No, she did, but very rarely. She always smiled rather than laughed. Not only did no one try to make her laugh, but whenever she laughed out loud, everyone looked at her in alarm. That's why I feel sad whenever I see Jini's smile, which people praise so much. It's not just me, but probably the whole family. Poor Jini. Wretched Jini. The sound of her laughter has never been recorded. After that day long ago, someone else's laughter was always used with her smiling face. Jini's laughter is always soundless. Like this. Her face is smiling, but there's no sound. Isn't that funny? And then silence swallowed all sounds. I think Jini was nine at the time, maybe ten.

Do I hate Jini? Not at all. I love Jini.

Lionfish

WHAT WAS SHOCKING, once again, was myself. The way I mourned the sudden death of someone who'd been so close to me, someone I thought I loved more than I loved myself until then. The way I bid her farewell, which couldn't be accepted unless your thoughts on love and happiness and joy were instantly overthrown.

D and I told each other about our pasts as we stayed up nights at the same laboratory, watching the results of experiments. I remember those nights by their ambience more than their substance, by truthful voices growing mistier as the night grew deeper, and the intense curiosity about each other that dispelled the desire to sleep. There's someone I want to stay up with all night, and that someone is you, I said, trying to win her love. But what was the use? What was the use of being together night and day for four years? What was the use of having made love, in the water, on the beach, on the table in a corner of the lab, in the corridor of a night train? She left, not knowing who I was after I turned in an instant into a stranger, without being able to do anything about it. That's what I saw in her eyes when I saw her for the last time. At first, there was resentment, at least, in her eyes. But then they grew cold.

"I always thought your nickname didn't suit you, but I just didn't know you. You are a lionfish after all. You have thirteen poisonous spines," she spat out one day and then left without looking back. That fight was so severe that it nearly put an end to our relationship. Lionfish was my nickname as a diver. She feared, and hated, the fish. The look of resentment when she hissed the insult at me didn't last more than ten seconds. Resentment is an emotion based on some kind of a bond, and its next stages are feelings of unfamiliarity and indifference. That day, too, she had gone through those stages. A moment of hot resentment, then those cold, glacier eyes.

She disappeared with a defensive look on her face, the kind you make when a complete stranger comes up to you to ask for directions. Someone you thought you knew well could turn into a stranger in an instant. People avoided taking a closer look because they were thrown off by the fact. Getting angry, bursting out crying, hating or resenting someone, these are all strategies of evasion. She grew cold, as if to say, I'm not going to try to evade this.

What shocked everyone was D's sudden death on the night of the wedding. I understand their shock. But my own reaction was incomprehensible, even to myself. It seemed as if someone else who was inside me was dealing coolly with the death and taking care of things for me, as if D's death had been predestined. I was the one who was most surprised at myself when I, without being the least bit ruffled, called the hospital, got in the ambulance with her, explained the situation in detail to the doctor with a clear mind, pushed away the effects of alcohol, took all the necessary steps after she was pronounced dead, and called her parents, whom I'd almost never talked to, informing them of her death. In this cold, graceful manner, I offered my condolences to her. It wasn't that I hadn't had any affection for her, or that I'd had a hunch about her death. How can I explain? It was as if . . . . Such efforts to explain are futile. In her death on the beach that night, I saw with a clarity that made such efforts to explain meaningless.

After the wedding, we drove to the beach, as we always did when we came to the island, and went to the little sandy shore near Hyeopjae, which D called "the watch beach." In May four years earlier, D had kissed me back on this beach and lost the watch I had brought her as a gift, a watch with detailed ornamentation around its face. D had taken the watch off and put it on top of a pile of clothes to go for a quick dip in the May sea. But the watch was gone when she came out, even though there had been no one else on the beach. We searched everywhere on the sandy shore, combing it thoroughly, but the watch was nowhere to be found. So whenever we went to Jeju Island, we went to the beach to 'look for the watch.' It was different that day. Neither D nor I brought up the watch, not even as a joke, nor did we kick the sand in jest. We kept up the appearance of newlyweds, which could be seen in countless numbers this season, as strictly as if we were adhering to some kind of a regulation. Tuxedo, wedding dress, bow tie, white gloves. There was a gentle breeze on the beach. The taste of the midday air, just getting warmed up, was sweet, and it was the perfect early autumn day. The sea was a deep blue, and it seemed as if we'd be able to see through the water to the view beneath the sea we'd seen the day before. It was probably the best weather we'd had that year. When D and I say that, of course, we mean the best weather for going underwater. But both D and I were awkwardly denying ourselves the desire to jump into the water, a desire our bodies expressed before our words did. It was as if we'd come to a tacit agreement never to jump into the sea together again.

We lacked only one thing then, a simple feeling of happiness. No one around us had told us how to be happy on such a special day, or how to express that happiness, so we stood awkwardly side by side, quietly looking at the sea. It seemed as if something was telling us that we shouldn't hold hands, we shouldn't kiss. It was as if a magnetic resistance had formed between us, making us repel each other.

We parked the car right there on the beach and sat down on the sand, sipping our drinks with a box of alcohol sitting in the open trunk. At first, we drank just a little. It hadn't even occurred to us yet to take off the suit and dress we had rented from a shop in Seoul. The sun was still warm, and D was careful not to get the dress soiled. We sat about three meters apart on the sand, our legs crossed. The distance between us was the psychological distance appropriate for people who had experienced something that couldn't be undone, the minimum distance required for them to think about the things they would have to face in the future. I only had the following words to say, or the following were the words that came out of my mouth: "Isn't the laundry fee included in the rental fee for the dress? Don't worry about it. We can relax."

D seemed to say something in reply, but her voice was swept away by the waves. I saw her posture relax momentarily. It was probably the natural effects of alcohol, not what I said. I heaved a sigh of relief.

There was something about the beauty of the sea that day that stimulated our thirst, though the sea usually does that. The rough wind from the horizon made us thirsty, and so did the seeds of anxiety sown in our bodies. Sipping our drinks, we watched the sun go down, and the feathery clouds spread out wide, turning red in the twilight, and the night, chilled by the wind, fell around us.

Up until evening, some villagers and children had gathered to see the newlyweds sitting on the sand, but the beach, with nothing to see at night, was completely empty now. We got to our feet, sensing the chill rise from the ground.

D and I were standing on the beach, each with a bottle of German white wine, a gift from a colleague. With one foot on top of a small boat, turned upside down and with the blue paint peeling, I was following the stimulation the alcohol created in my body. I saw D whip her veil off and tie her hair back. By then, we were both getting deeply drunk. I didn't know how many bottles there'd been at the beginning, but the box in the open car trunk was being filled with empty bottles. I knew why we had come to the beach. So did D. We wanted to confirm something without saying anything. But neither D nor I could bring up what had happened underwater the day before.

We kept holding off the truth in this way, and then D drowned, on the night of our wedding. The cause of death, as determined by the doctor who'd come running from the emergency room of a nearby hospital, was a heart attack. The physical causes of deaths are often put in abstruse terms. But the cause of D's death was quite simple.

A large star caught my eye as I looked up at the sky while watching the repetitive but addicting movements of the white waves continuously crashing into the dark blue surface, then backing away. I don't know the location or the name of the star, as I'm ignorant of the world of gases and solids in the sky, in the universe. When I slowly lowered my gaze, which had been hanging in space for a moment, I saw an enormous white morning glory, its petals spread wide on the surface of the undulating dark blue water. I shook my head violently. It really was a morning glory. It wasn't just the effects of the alcohol that made me see the flower sink beneath the dark surface, leaving behind a faint, indistinct afterimage. When I managed to see D in her wedding dress in that afterimage, it was too late.

What had made me just stand and watch it happen? When I walked into the water, I was shocked by the depth of the shallow sea, reaching just above my knees. She came up on my shoulder, reproaching me with the weight of her body, swollen with water. I don't know if such things could be called fate. Could it be that D's star had been there to see her off as she prepared to leave this earth?

If only we hadn't drunk, if only I hadn't looked up to see the star, if only the mysterious star that had held my eyes had let me go, even just one moment earlier, if only I had run to get her out of the water instead of watching the curves of her white dress turn into a vanishing afterimage on the dark surface . . . . All the ifs were meaningless. The virtue of a heart attack lies in instantaneous arrival. The death of the body takes place before the death of the mind.

If I were in D's shoes, I probably would have made a similar decision. I, too, would have walked drunk into the night sea, with no other plans, or intent, to die. There aren't forty-four reasons as to why one walks into the sea. There is only one reason. The cause of D's death is suicide, not drowning due to heart attack, as stated on the diagnosis in the emergency room, I thought. Not suicide as intended, but suicide that finds its way in naturally as the thing that sustains life is exhausted. What had sustained D? I know it wasn't me. It was something I didn't know about, something that must have become clear to her because of what had happened that day. That's how I saw D's death. The only thing that could determine whether it had been an accident or a suicide was the fact that the water wasn't deep enough to commit suicide in. No matter how much I thought about it, D's death, by nature, had been inevitable. What else could she have done when she witnessed herself being denied like that? The effects of alcohol on us had been sinister.

D left the world having learned nothing from me, because I myself didn't know what had happened. Even if she'd asked,

I couldn't have answered. It was only much later that I remembered how the image of the woman D and I had seen underwater had overlapped with the faint afterimage of D, who went down into the water, a white flower from the dark and vast surface at night, and that it was because of this image, which came to my mind at the moment D's afterimage was vanishing, that I couldn't move.

That day, we became paralyzed by what had appeared in the fantastic light, filtered by the brilliant sunlight, as we looked up to the surface while ascending through the water—by the form, by the face, by what had emanated from the body. Both D and I realized that we'd seen the most dazzling thing in the world at that moment, with no time for the bitter emptiness, filling our mouths little by little, to settle. The premonition, felt thereafter, that the world would now be a very different place was what pulled us apart. That more than the incident itself.

Shark

I'M TURNING TWENTY-TWO soon. I don't believe in anything. I don't want a soul inside my body. I gave up family, friends, books, and school early on. I learned that things like that aren't what you need in order to survive in this world. Roaming around in the marketplace from a young age, you come to learn something: that everything that has a soul is corrupt. The days of pure, innocent souls are past. All that the rest of mankind can hope for in this backward age is to be subject to less destruction. Sometimes I prefer inanimate objects over organisms, and inorganic matter over organic. I'm going to stop aging when I'm twenty-two. I've experienced everything that's worth experiencing by people older than that. How tedious life would be if life after twenty-two was nothing more than a repetition of what you've already done before. Knowing that, why grow older and become an adult? I hate kids, but I think it's the greatest disaster to become an adult. I'm not talking about actual age. Those who know, know what I'm talking about. Those who want to pretend they don't can do as they please.

But unfortunately, the characteristics of adulthood manifest themselves in relation to one's age, so actual age, in reality, isn't altogether irrelevant.

What it comes down to is that I'm not going to grow any older. I'm old enough as it is at twenty-two. From now on, I'm

not going to carry around any identification card that proves
who I am. I'm going to go on journeys without my ID, and I'm
going to drive without my driver's license. I promise myself that
today, two months and eight days since Jini left me.

The things people do are offensive and ugly to me. Why do
they get up in the morning and go to bed at night? Why do they
think something terrible will happen if they don't have three
meals a day? Why do they smile and say hello to everyone they
meet and say things that are different from what they're thinking, without ever reflecting on what they do? Why do they meet
someone they hate and fail to express their feelings for someone
they love? Why do they get married when their smooth skin
turns rough, and have children when they're married, and buy
a house when they have children, and fill up their house with
ugly and boring things? Why can't you beat and break things
when you're furious, or set fire to something when you're angry
and disappointed, or kill someone when you hate him? Why do
these others cling to people they hate, and say goodbye to people
they love? I despise people who've come up with all these rules.

What I like are simple things. I like all sensations that expand.
I don't believe in anything I can't confirm by touching, and I
don't acknowledge the existence of anything that doesn't bring
pleasure. I'm a presentist. That's the compass of my life. These
are the things I like just now, but given more time, the list will
grow infinitely. I like those moments when I'm reduced to a
fleshy lump of sensation, when sensation expands to eliminate
the mind. I feel eternity in those moments. I don't particularly
like that sentence, but that's a fact, and has to be stated that way.
An empty eternity where I'm in exile. I like riding up mountain
slopes at breakneck speed, with the motor revved into the red.
It's worth a try to stick your head out of the water just before you
pass out. I express my hatred for the world through my body,

as if in a dance. I despise artificial manipulation of the senses through drugs and alcohol. I advocate for all sensations that are expanded without that stuff. I like Jini's silence as well. I like empty silence that doesn't convey anything. I really like Jini's body, which doesn't express anything through words, words, words. I know that I'll die in a state in which my sensations extend to their greatest potential. But I could end up living for a long time, even if that's not something I want.

To stop time when I'm twenty-two, I plan to buy a desert island. This is still far off, but I'll come up with a way to own an island. I'll stay in this world only until I have one. There was a time when I was obsessed with possessing things. I was immature. But I don't regret it.

On the island, I'm going to start, at age twenty-two, the second phase of my life. I can't say if it'll be long or short. I'm not going to take anyone or anything with me to the island. If Jini comes back . . . I haven't really thought about that yet. I'm going to take a long break there, without music or family or friends. There will be no children being born because there will be no adult there aside from myself. I could die, isolated on the island, through a typhoon, tsunami, or another unexpected natural disaster. That's something I would like. I would live to die of a natural disaster on a desolate island surrounded by dark blue sea. I've looked into one or two desert islands. I'll probably buy one of those islands that aren't even on the map.

After Jini's disappearance, this plan became my only clear idea. I didn't tell anyone about it, even though it had been on my mind for quite some time. And yet, I happened to tell Jini on the way back from the shoot the day before she left. But I told her only because the shooting location was a small desert island. I'm not sure if she heard me even, because she was looking out the window with a completely dazed look on her face as usual.

Jini's absence put out the light of the world for me. But I don't hate this dark world.

I'll need money to buy an island. I still have time. And Jini isn't coming back.

Agar-Agar

IT WAS IMPOSSIBLE for the woman, who was so quick of hearing, not to hear the door open and close that early morning two months ago. She had the kind of ears that only someone who was abandoned as a child and had to wander from place to place as a teenager has, someone who was anxious about basic survival, the kind of ears that were as sensitive as animal ears. She had five children but lost two of them when they were little. It was a very long time ago. One was a girl, who died from carbon monoxide poisoning in a room whose door was locked from the outside. The girl was two-and-a-half years old, and the woman was selling cabbages at a corner at the marketplace downtown with an even younger child on her back and no one at home. The death of the second child occurred soon after the birth. He must have lasted about an hour. The boy had been born within a year of the birth of the oldest surviving girl.

For a long time, she went on blaming herself for not having heard the cry of her daughter while she shouted, "Take home some Chinese cabbages!" Whenever she thought back to that moment, she couldn't free herself of the thought that she'd sensed something strange but ignored it. Back then, she was young and afraid of having another mouth to feed. But there's no chance that she could have heard the cry of the two-and-a-half-year-old girl. It was only something she wished had happened. The marketplace where she worked was at least an hour away from the rented room where her family lived. For some time, she would punish herself in her own way, going out without wearing winter clothes or not going to bed at night even as she dozed. But all unfortunate memories became diluted with the passage of time. She didn't remember much about the second child she'd lost. Around that time, she was somewhat older, but was still living in deep poverty and giving birth was still something to worry about, whether it was to a boy or a girl. The misfortune didn't end with the loss of the two children, but three of the children survived, and with the birth of the youngest, she finally reached a point where she didn't need to worry about their survival. The memory of her husband, who'd now been dead for six or seven years, turned into a dark spot in her mind, blocking a part of her brain without bringing sorrow or remorse. The woman believed that everyone lived to their fullest, and she didn't feel a sense of injustice at the length of anyone's life.

There was a reason, however, as to why her hearing had developed so remarkably. For her ears became even more sensitive after the most painful incident in her life, which she failed to make peace with. The incident, which could not be verified, had honed her hearing to the most precise degree. And because the woman tried to verify a sound that couldn't be verified, she came to pay more attention to the sounds of the world, with greater frequency and sensitivity. Her hearing wasn't as good as when the children were younger and she could hear them crying even far away, but her ears still worked like a finely tuned instrument. She could hear every sound in the world, and because she was so absorbed in these sounds, she often appeared absent in this world.

The woman thought she could hear the sound of heaven, the sound underground, the sounds resonating in the air, the

sounds in the distance, in faraway cities. At least, she heard incessant rumblings that she assumed were these sounds. She could
hear the ground cracking under her foot, something collapsing
and breaking in the distance, and the clamoring things deep
underground as they surged back and forth, all as if they came
from very close. Her mind was always someplace else, where the
sounds took her.

So that early morning, she heard the door open and close.
But she lay there without stirring, her heart pounding with the
fear that the others may awaken. She felt at peace now. She felt
anxious, but at peace. So again, she packed her backpack and
got ready to climb a mountain. This time, she would stay several
days.

She packed the things she needed in her backpack. Two pairs
of underwear, side dishes, condiments, a muffler that would protect her exceptionally thin neck, a woolen hat. Lastly, she stuffed
a fabric bag full of rolled up plastic sheets into the backpack.
She stuffed the old backpack as if she were going hiking in midwinter. She put on the goose-down winter parka her youngest
daughter had bought her. It was early winter. The temperature
in the mountains around the end of November was low. She
knew that the mountains cooled down earlier than the hour of
sunset as announced by the weather service, between four and
five. At the moment when the sun went down, she always barely
managed to suppress a desire to howl like animals on a foggy
mountain, in warning of the impending darkness.

Before she got on the bus, the woman bought two thick
candles at the shop in front of the bus station. You need light
on the mountain at night. The woman preferred candles over
a flashlight. She got on the bus and dozed off, because she had
tossed and turned all night. In her dreams, she had a fight with
someone, shoving and getting shoved. The person seemed to

be her son, or her husband. They kept their faces shielded, so she couldn't tell who the other person was, but she fought with all the strength she had. When dawn came around, she sat up, fuming. When she opened her eyes, the person who'd clung to her all night like a leech melted away into the light of the dawn. The woman opened the door and shouted, "Get out!", but no voice came out, so she kept motioning with her hand to chase him away, and went on motioning.

But the woman opened her eyes and got off at the station right in front of the mountain. She began climbing up. It was a weekday, so there weren't many hikers. She climbed fast, as if she'd mastered the magic art of covering distances. From far away, it probably looked as if she were dancing. She had a lightness and flexibility uncharacteristic of a woman who was nearing fifty. She stopped before a little boulder, gasping, and laughed while looking at the hazy city down below. Oh, it's so funny, oh, oh! She laughed, smacking her lips even. Countless images of the affairs of the world came to her mind, then disappeared.

The woman started climbing again. She came to a stop not too far from the summit, frowning and perking her ears. She heard people murmuring, a sound almost like wailing, coming from everywhere on the mountain. She called it the sound of prayer. She could tell the mountains apart by certain tones, certain energies that came from the amalgamation of sounds. She had an unfortunate knack for going in a direction she shouldn't take in life. The woman, afraid, didn't choose. She went anywhere, without any criteria. That day, too, she began climbing toward the summit, randomly taking a trail on the western side. So with only two breaks, she reached the summit.

The morning sun had just barely gone over the top of the mountain as she looked east from the summit, but already there were two other women there, sitting back to back on a rock, pouring out incoherent prayers as if competing with each other. On another rock, a man sat with his head hanging low. The two women moved their upper bodies from left to right to the same rhythm, but then one of them raised her head as Agar-Agar approached them, saying, "You're here!".

"Yeah, you got here early. I'll see you later," she answered abruptly in a husky voice. She ran into someone she knew no matter which valley she went to. It had been nearly ten years since she started coming here. She picked a rock far away from them. Narrowing her eyes, she bent down and measured the height of the rock against the sky. The rock she picked looked even taller against the sky. She climbed and sat on the rock, as if to say, this is good enough. She pulled the parka tighter around herself, put on the muffler and hat, took out her thermos and poured herself hot tea, and then blew on it in between sips. She tidied up the things in the backpack, and began the griping she calls prayer. At first she thought the word gido (prayer) referred to gido (airway), and loved it. She had long been desperate to breathe without hindrance. Now that she'd been coming to the mountains for some time, not only was she familiar with others who came, but she was also quite eloquent, with a richer vocabulary. She enjoyed using the words she'd picked up here and there in different valleys. She whispered something incoherent for a long time, and finally raised her voice. It was in the tone of a command:

"Listen to my cries! There's Namsan to the south, Seoraksan to the east, Hallasan down below, Baekdusan to the north, Jirisan in the middle, Everest farther away, Kilimanjaro on that southern continent, Mont Blanc far away in the west, let my cries spread throughout the celebrated mountains around the world, and communicate with all the people praying like us, that the world may be happy . . . ."

The woman's hoarse voice, which wasn't any slighter than the firm, strong voices of others praying at the summit, was buried in the loud cacophony of voices of people wishing for their children's health, successful investment in securities, a husband's promotion, sales of apartments, recovery from sickness, a son's marriage, a daughter's divorce, a mistress's instant death, a nephew's entrance examination, and so forth. The woman at times whispered, and at times raised her voice in command or indignation, began to sway back and forth and right to left, her eyes closed, and then gradually began to lose herself in prayer like the others:

"Who knows about the misfortune that fell on a family in northeast Seoul yesterday? I am here to tell the world about the atrocious thing that's happened. Why did a thing like this happen to that poor family? A whole family was massacred for no reason. The son, still wet behind the ears, did it using spikes and a hammer. All because of money. Killed each and every person in the family, without even blinking his eyes. Oh, let punishment fall upon him, let severe punishment fall upon him that such a thing may not happen again on earth! Yes, it's just that punishment fall upon him. And I keep thinking about the couple who got swept up in the current while seeking pleasure in the car with their child sleeping in the tent during the flood last year. Oh, it must be because of the child that I keep thinking about them, the child who got swept away in the water. Poor things, wretched things, damned things, the child who died in the flooded tent was so young. I wonder if the child was taken to the beautiful heavenly garden, the poor things, the relentless things, I pray and pray that the child may be saved. I pray with my two hands folded together."

The woman's cry continued on in a high pitch, as if she were talking to a neighbor, or to herself. She stopped now and then to spit next to the rock, then resumed her impassioned speech.

"Today I pray especially for all the poor people who died fighting or died hungry on the many continents on earth. Let the cries of the lonely spread throughout this boundless earth. Save me and save them, good for good and evil for evil, and comfort this heart full of bitterness. I give thee all their names, so take their hands, one by one, and sit them down around thee . . . ."

The woman shouted out the names quickly and without reserve, even when she could recall only the last names, until the morning sun warmed the top of her head. Her voice grew hushed with certain names, as if she were chanting a secret. Quite a number of foreign names also made their way into the prayer. From time to time, she took out a piece of crumpled paper from her bag, and blinking her bleary eyes, she rattled off the names she'd written down in awkward handwriting, along with the stories that went with the names.

The struggle continued throughout the morning, as dictated by the images flashing across her mind. The woman called out the names of people who'd become victims of the collapse, immorality, injustice, and corruption of the world, from the north to the south of the Korean Peninsula, as well as from the east to the west, and all around the world. She even wept bitterly at times, for herself, who counted among them. Occasionally she sipped some hot tea, and choking with tears at times and sobbing at times, she cried out desperately as if the unfortunate people whose names she called out were right before her eyes. Another woman, who'd been crying out just as sharply, came over and took a hold of her sleeve and she finally came out of her trance in which time went on without her.

"Why don't you come eat with us?"

The small group, gathered from this valley and that, sat down in a spacious cavity of a huge rock that kept the wind out and spread out their packed lunches. Cooked rice, kimchi, beef boiled down in soy sauce, cucumber kimchi, cubed-radish kimchi, stir-fried anchovies, laver, apples, tangerines, and salted fish were spread out on the ground at random.

"Any news of your daughter?"

"No!" she spat out gruffly, pursing her lips.

"Nothing's going to happen, so you can all rest easy," she said.

"It's not that we want to worry—we just feel sorry for you."

She turned to the other woman, saying, "Why would you feel sorry for me? What a damned thing to say."

"You've got a pretty face, but a foul mouth."

They polished off the food in a flash and each had a bottle of yogurt that had come out of someone's bag. They poured instant coffee mix into the tea in the thermos to share, and then returned to their spots after taking a sip each. This time, the woman sat up straight facing east, and with her eyes closed, began to whisper to a four-count rhythm:

"Old days gone by, old world gone by, before the night comes to an end, sad and bitter tales will be told throughout the world, truth will come forth, the world will shine, the animals, as well as plants, will come to life, human fate will be decided, and every bitter heart will be healed, and what is broken will be mended, all the struggles will be resolved, all hell will end, and the wicked will be punished, birds with flowers will fly in the sky, the promised day will be ushered in, the sad, sad world will come to an end, these poor, dim eyes will see clearly, with the water from the valley on a spring day, the corrupt world will be as clean as the water underground, the decrepit human body will be as pure as a baby's, and as soft and warm and strong, too, hush my baby, hush, hush, baby . . . ."

The woman's voice subsided, and her words became jumbled together without meaning. The sun was setting already and people were beginning to climb back down the mountain. When the darkness fell suddenly, as it does on the mountains, only two people remained at the summit. There was the woman, and another woman about her age, who came carrying her backpack and limping, her legs stiff from sitting in the same position for a long time.

"Are you going to stay the night?" the other woman asked.

"Yeah. Bring your plastic sheet. I'll wrap it around you."

The two women sat down in a dent among the rocks, their bodies stiff and numb. The woman took out two candles from her backpack and lit them. Finally, she took out the lump of plastic sheet from the other woman's backpack, wrapped it carefully around her six or seven times, and tied it up so it wouldn't come undone. Then she took out her own plastic sheet from her backpack and wrapped it around herself. The two women looked like standing cocoons. They looked at each other and burst out laughing, and went on laughing until they were teary-eyed. They brought their hands, with which they'd been wrapping the plastic sheet around themselves, inside the cocoon, and began their night of prayer. They could now stay up all night without getting frostbitten, even if there was a fierce night wind. And even if they dozed off while praying, they would live to see the morning sunrise.

Conch

MY NAME IS Kim Chanhee, and I'm waiting for Jini. The person who wishes more desperately than anyone else in the world for Jini's return is me, Conch, or Kim Chanhee. Everyone else in the family is only pretending to wait. I am—and my waiting is—different. It can be compared to the waiting of someone trying to sort out what she truly believes in her final hours. And I have the right to do so.

I met Jini eight years ago, and it took me six years to make Jini who she is today. No one in this family will object to that. No one knows the passion, the agony, the pain, and the joy that went into molding Jini. These were all mine, and the fact that they were mine and mine alone is the reason for my existence. If the pain was great, the joy was twice as great. If there was agony, it was a triviality that vanished once Jini smiled. Jini is my family and my universe, my work, my love, my child. I know the joy of creation. Jini is the source of all my joy. I have never encountered a body with such expressions, lines, and volume as I've found in Jini's—a body that brings perfect pleasure. I've never met anyone who can create the kind of ambience Jini does when she moves or immerses herself in creating an expression and corresponding inner essence.

I made Jini who she is today, but it would only be fair to say that Jini, too, made me who I am. I've become who I am now together with Jini, and through her mastered a knowledge no one else could have. I am considerate enough, and respectful enough, to acknowledge that.

Before we met, Jini was just Yi Jina, and I was just Kim Chanhee. After we met, she became Jini, and I became Conch. One day, she wrote on my palm. "Can I call you Conch?" I nodded my head, or course. On Jini's palm, which at the time was still sweetly small and delicate, I wrote down and whispered in her ear, "Yes, from now on, I'm your Conch." I wasn't used to our silent conversations yet.

By the time she gave me the name, people said her speech impediment was already well developed. I think she would still say one or two words now and then, but I'm not sure if I remember correctly. In any case, I was already a guest and a part of her family, living in one of the rooms at the house.

Writing on palms was our way to communicate. I loved it when Jini's slender finger drew little circles and lines and dots on my palm. The advantage of this palm language was that it made us say only what was absolutely necessary. As time passed, we didn't even have to finish a word. As with shorthand, Jini and I could read each other's messages with the first consonant alone. The rest of our communication was done through our mouths and eyes. I learned how to read Jini's eyes, and Jini learned how to read the movements of my lips. But in most cases, I didn't even have to read her eyes. I could read all her changes, all her sorrows and joys in detail, as if there was something emanating from Jini with scents and colors and shapes. That's the kind of relationship we had.

To be honest, I miss the days when Jini's little chubby fingers drew awkward letters on my palm. How I long to go back to

that time. I learned maternal love through Jini. If Agar-Agar's
maternal love was animal and primitive, the maternal love I
poured out on Jini, I dare say, was prudent and rational. It was
beyond camaraderie or sisterhood. So how could Jini not say
anything to me when she left this house? That is the question
that haunts me the most now that she's not here. When did the
understanding between us begin to rupture?

When I first met Jini, I didn't need much time to see the
famous child model in the brightly smiling little girl.

Before she met me, Jini was a little girl attending elementary school, one who was somewhat lazy and didn't like school.
She was the youngest daughter of clumsy and ignorant parents
who were still struggling with life, although they'd just begun to
extricate themselves from poverty through the money the child
brought in as an advertising model. I wasn't any better off than
they were, really. I'd just lost my boyfriend and my job and was
having an even harder time dealing with being on my own since
leaving my father's home after my parents' divorce.

It took another year for my life and Jini's to be tied together
in a tight knot. After I quit my job, I took on several temporary
positions as people do in my field of work. I was a little tired,
and one afternoon when the city was covered in yellow dust, I
went to see Jini. It wasn't just coincidence. The first time I met
Jini, I took her home, and I went to see her again because I had
some business to attend to in the neighborhood. The reason I
went to see her, though, was because I wanted to feel strengthened again by the smile she sent my way the first time we'd met.
I only meant to spend an hour or two with Jini after school,
but the smile a year before must have been fateful for me, for
I became a part of her family after that. At first I just rented a
room in their house, but the year after that, I willingly took on
the role of raising and training Jini. In that small and shabby

house that doesn't even compare to the house we live in now, my dreams and joy began to grow. The area has since turned into a shopping district, with no trace of the old house, but I pass through every so often with inconsolable nostalgia.

I believe that I brought Jini good luck. It goes without saying that Jini herself was good luck for me. I never forget those who show me kindness. After I began to live with Jini, a lot of good things happened to both of us. Jini became busy and evolved into who she is today, and I got to do what I'd always wanted to do. Things weren't always good, of course. Jini's father, for instance, passed away just before I began to live in the house. But is the death of someone only a misfortune? No one can say for sure. Sometimes in my dreams, all of us—Shark, Starfish, Agar-Agar, and I—turn into carnivores who feed on Jini's body. But Jini's small body doesn't shrink or disappear, so our feeding continues in my dreams.

On the day I met Jini for the first time, I'd just been betrayed and abandoned by a man. At twenty-five, I was young and inexperienced. I was working three days a week at the media library of an educational institution on the outskirts of the city. My job consisted mostly of organizing and lending the tapes in the library. Three times a week, I put the returned tapes in order, and categorized and displayed new materials, adding titles and brief information about them. I was checking a new linguistic program that had come in that day when the man hastily approached me without notice. He was the head of my department, whom I'd been seeing for two years. He said to me in an angry tone, as hastily as he'd approached, "Miss Kim, I need to talk to you for a minute."

Both the tone of his voice and the formality of his address foretold the drastic and ludicrous nature of what was about to take place. Comically enough, the words "Do you love me?" were repeating over and over again in different intonations on the English learning tape that was playing.

I followed him to a hill in a mountain valley. There was a little stone seat there, where he and I had sat fighting and whispering words of love. I don't remember exactly what words he used. But the point was that he was seeing someone else, so we shouldn't see each other anymore. He didn't add any explanation that I could understand, and the whole time he looked irritated, as if to say he basically hated human relationships that required such explanations in order to end them.

Saying nothing more he went down the hill, and I began to cry with my face buried in my hands. I was watching him through my fingers, but he left the small valley without looking back once, and when he disappeared out of view, I buried my face deeper in my arms.

It's a scene I don't want to recall. But I'm not concerned anymore with the puppy love that came to an end after two years. What I want to talk about is the encounter that led me to a world that gave meaning to my life. That encounter brings me the same joy no matter how many times I talk about it.

I lifted my face, sensing that someone was watching me. A girl was standing in the shadow of a tree off to the side, smiling dazzlingly at me. No one had been there just a moment before, but the girl, whose skirt was rolled up so high that her tiny underwear showed through, was watching me, kicking at the water with her foot. Her exceptionally thin, perfect nape caught my eyes. The girl, still watching me, put on the green linen shirt she'd taken off and came toward me. Then in an awkward and unclear voice she said to me, "Don't cry. Did someone hurt you?"

I don't remember exactly what kind of tone her voice took on at that moment, but I remember that it was gentle and that it washed away my sorrow. What I recall vividly, however, are the words she spoke to me:

"Did someone squeeze your neck?"

These words, which I'd forgotten about for a long time, come to my mind with a completely new meaning now that Jini is no longer at my side. When she was with me, I didn't need to think about her. Jini was my thought itself. The words I'd dismissed as the meaningless babble of a little girl have taken on a somewhat clearer meaning after the seven years of my living with her. Had she perhaps been asking me for help, smiling so brightly? I was immature, and drunk in my own sorrow, and had missed the hidden message in the shadow of her smile. Now that Jini isn't with me, the irredeemable regret of the past is rushing back to me as a whirlwind of pain.

I am waiting for Jini. She will come back. She will stand in front of me one day, smiling that smile of hers—in a completely unexpected moment, in the same way she came to talk to me that first time—when I'm walking in a daze around the corner of a street, or when I close my eyes for a moment and open them again. We will revel together in pure happiness. You can't turn around when happiness is just ahead and act as if it doesn't exist. That's not the way of Conch, or Kim Chanhee. I'm waiting for Jini. I'm going to find Jini.

Part Two

What she remembers is the single descent.

The infinite relief in her body from the temperature, color, and feel of the water.

Perhaps her plans to leave were already in place the moment she went underwater, with a nearly perfect faith, as if she were descending into the womb of Agar-Agar.

One Day, She Was Out the Door

ONE MORNING, SHE woke up to the sound of music passing under the window. She looked out to see the back of a boy, walking into the woods with a portable audio player in his hand on that warm spring day. The boy's pants were hiked up to his knees and he had a fishing net in his other hand, as if he'd just come out of a stream where he'd been fishing. Where had she seen this image before? It was one of those pleasant images that came to her mind from time to time. She'd never seen the boy's face, of course. But she remembered his jaunty gait, as well as the small, red audio player and the fast song flowing out of the device. She remembered the woods growing darker after the boy went inside. Everything that flowed, everything that was transparent, made her happy. Many things flowed, but not many were transparent. And many transparent things did not flow. She knew a light came on in her body when sounds, water, and air began to flow together. She was always ready to call out to them. They made her skin breathe, accelerated the flow of her blood, and brought her the pleasure of oblivion. That was her weapon. When she was out of breath, when her heart was breaking, she could disappear. When she closed her eyes and smiled, she was somewhere else, in an image or scene that made her happy. She could go to sleep in this way anytime, anywhere.

When she opened her eyes again, she began to hear the sound
of rain instead of the sound of music. She realized that it was
time for her to leave. It just was; she would have known it if it
was yesterday, or tomorrow. The sound of the rain had nothing
to do with her decision to leave all that she was familiar with. A
rainy day isn't the best day to set out on a journey. But she didn't
mind the rain. Rain wasn't in the picture during the dozens, or
perhaps hundreds, of times when she thought about leaving.
But her hesitation didn't last long and wasn't strong enough to
overturn her decision.

The decision was made instantly. It was that day. She looked
back with a quiet sadness on her life up to then, not too long, as
you do when you've made an unwitting mistake. Several familiar faces flashed before her eyes, but she lightly waved goodbye
to them.

Actually, she couldn't even understand why she felt sad. She
wasn't unhappy, nor was she happy. She'd always had to throw
herself into the work that came in incessantly, so she never had
the time to think about such things as happiness or unhappiness.
For a long time, in fact, devoting herself to the basic survival
of those around her had been the source of her little happiness.
But now, she'd done what she could. The faces that pulled at her
didn't have enough power to make her change her mind. Her
thoughts rested for a moment on Agar-Agar's face, and she realized that her sadness came from that face. But she was vaguely
aware that neither she nor Agar-Agar, or anyone else for that
matter, could do anything about the sadness. It was an inevitable
sorrow that took a hold of her when she thought back to the
moment of her birth, the moment when she fell into the world.

Dawn was approaching, but it was still night. Night wasn't a
good time to set out on a journey, either. But she'd never imagined that she would set out on her journey at any other time.

She had most often pictured herself walking on a spring night with an overcast moon. But her springs had always been busy, so she had had no time to think about leaving. And at night, she had to try and get some sleep, comforting her body, anxious with the things it had to accomplish the next day. Spring would come around again and again, so it didn't really matter. She wasn't that particular.

It wouldn't be right to say that she made up her mind to set out on her journey all of a sudden. She knew that she wasn't the only one who had had a hand in her leaving. For some time, someone in the family had been opening up the locked door late at night. There were only four other people living in the house, and she didn't want to know which of them it was. The person locking the door and the person opening it up again could, of course, be one and the same. But common sense tells you that someone who opens a door does not think in the same way that someone who locks a door does. Who snuck out in the middle of the night, when everyone was asleep, to open up all the locked doors?

If the hand belonged to Starfish, she might have been sneaking out late at night to go running in the empty streets of the city. Jini pictured Starfish, shrieking and darting into the street. She was aware of Starfish's insomnia. Or Starfish might have been driving all night on a wet road. Jini could no longer accompany Starfish on her trips to the end of the night. Or was it Conch? If it was, Conch would have waited for her every night outside the door. How intensely had Conch wanted to go on a trip with her. Conch had wanted a trip for just the two of them, a pivotal trip, the kind they could never have again. What if it was? If it was Conch? Jini didn't go on thinking for long. She suddenly realized who it was that had opened the locked door late at night, the significance of that little gesture. She recalled the faint smile that came on Agar-Agar's face when she was sober, her eyes closed.

Yes, that must be it.

She pulled out a suitcase from under the bed. She realized that she'd been planning this trip for a very long time. Whenever she felt like it, she would put something she'd need in the suitcase before going to bed. All she had to do now was to put those things, mixed up together in the suitcase, in order. Next to the blue, train-patterned suitcase she took with her when she went on a photo tour, there was another one of the same color and design, hidden deep under the bed.

She left no traces before leaving. She didn't remove any traces, either. The whiteboard hanging on the wall by her bedside was crammed with schedules. As always, she looked with indifference at her heavy schedule, which she'd never complained about, and which she'd always carried out without difficulty. She left things the way they were. She didn't, for example, erase her schedule.

The long training that went on for hours every day with Conch and Shark watching was part of her schedule. She would practice breathing, walking, smiling, raising her hands, and making expressions countless times. Or she would try on accessories and outfits over and over again. There were long lists of things she couldn't eat, things she couldn't do. She went through with the busy, futile routine without any complaint. She knew that there would come a time when none of it would matter, and perhaps they did, too. But in this world, useful things, though very few in number, happened because of futile gestures. She knew what people wanted. Sitting quietly among people, she would come upon the essence of things. She would become the state, the boundary, the subject she needed to portray. She herself couldn't tell how it happened. So it was a secret even to herself.

In the final phase of a shooting, she always returned to this moment. But the long and repetitive practices weren't entirely meaningless. There are people who need the existence of certain things in order to confirm that they're alive. She willingly became those things for them. She looked at the disorderly pile of materials leaning against a wall. There were recordings about her, with titles and dates meticulously written down by Conch. Goodbye, dark tapes. She didn't include any of them on the list of things to put in her suitcase.

Poor Conch. The person she thought of on the morning she left wasn't Agar-Agar, or Shark, or Starfish. She remained feeling sorry for a moment for Conch, who'd changed the course of her own life along with her, and because of her. Conch always wanted things she couldn't have. Things that didn't seem mere coincidences often happened to Conch. When Conch wished for a bright, clear day, it was always cloudy the next day. None of the men Conch wanted reciprocated her feelings. The things Conch wanted were always out of her reach, and because she was adamant, what she wanted could never be hers. Conch wanted to be happy, but the desire was so intense and absolute that it became the cause of her trouble. Conch was always unhappy because of her need for happiness. Goodbye, Conch. When will I see you again? she wondered.

She hadn't even left the room yet, but already the room was no longer hers. The room had never been hers. Nothing in the world had ever been hers. She, the youngest daughter of Agar-Agar, had never been Agar-Agar's daughter. She didn't know what that meant. Sometimes she wondered how she came to have such close and intense relationships with all these people. All she had in common with them were trifling things: a certain gesture at times; a certain part of the face or the shape of a foot; fingernails.

But she could have met them somewhere else, not under the same roof. She could have met them in an alleyway, or sat down next to one of them on a train, and come to live with them and to love them as Conch had done. That's what love meant to her. She couldn't go back on her decision to leave because of such love. Soon, they would forget her absence. There's nothing in the world you can't get over.

But . . . if someone had woken up and tried to stop her as she opened the door to her room, then the front door, and then as she went out the gate, she might have returned to her room. They would have told her in all sincerity about the dangers of going out in this way, and she would have come back, not because she agreed that it was dangerous, but because that person's desire to stop her would have been stronger than her own desire to leave. That was the kind of journey she was going to undertake. She would leave without any plans, simply because the time for her to leave had come. It didn't matter when she set out.

For her, in fact, it didn't matter where she went. She had no fantasies about home or the street, outside or inside. She had learned that very early on. And for that reason, she would have come back without any resistance. And she would have played the role assigned her, according to schedule as usual. She could have grown up in that way, from a famous young model to a mature woman, and become even more renowned, then forgotten as her body began to wither. She could have died as one of those people. For her, death had always seemed a light relief after a long, hard struggle.

Things, however, unfolded in a different way. It was very strange. As she opened and closed the three doors—the door to her room, the front door, and the gate—no one woke up. Having only followed someone in or out, she was surprised that the doors she had believed were always locked at night opened so easily, and that there was no resistance involved in going out those doors. The doors all slid open silently, as if equipped with a sound-absorbing mechanism. It wasn't the door, however, that astounded her. It was a faceless mannequin that had always stood in a corner of the living room. A part of her top got caught on one of the mannequin's arms, stretched out in a strange, awkward pose, and she nearly fell to the floor along with the bulky plaster body. Conch would always hang the things Jini had to wear that day on the mannequin, which had been there for as long as she could remember. She couldn't recall when the mannequin's head had broken off. Starfish had drawn on the face with a black colored pencil, two large teardrops that didn't trickle down. A piece of coarse metal that used to connect the head to the body protruded from where the head had been. She quietly untangled her top and went past the mannequin.

That was all. Nothing special happened. If she walked quietly, it was just her habit. She always walked quietly when she wasn't in front of the camera, as if she wanted to fold herself up as small as possible and carry herself in her pocket. She didn't hesitate once as she went through the three doors. She had no plans she had to carry out. She had simply made up her mind to go outside, as if coming inside. Now that she thought about it, it was the first time she'd ever gone out these doors with no one leading her way.

So it wasn't because of disappointment or hope that she left home early that morning. She didn't pick up her suitcase because of anger, expectation, hatred, or forgiveness. She didn't have anything special to find, and she had nothing to lose, either. She had nothing she had to see or forget. If everything had happened differently in the first place, of course, there would have been no reason for her to leave. Just as she wouldn't have existed if she

hadn't been born. Leaving wouldn't have been a decision she had
to make. But things happened and came to her that way, and she
knew deep inside that starting over was meaningless. Stirring up
a tranquil pool of water had nothing to do with her leaving. She
decided that this was how it happened: she heard the sound of
music passing through under the window in the rain, and went
outside without planning to do so.

She opened the front door, put on her shoes, turned the
doorknob, and heard her heart pounding. It thumped as if it
had just begun to exist at that moment. The sound frightened
her for a moment. Then she saw the gate at the end of the yard,
looking distant as if it were somewhere that couldn't be reached.
She walked across the yard, full of weeds that had turned yellow
as the year drew to an end, and which were getting wet in the
autumn rain.

And then she was outside. She took off her shoes, and ran
barefoot in the rain until she was out of breath and could no longer run. Only then did she realize that there had been no sound
of music anywhere, and that the image of herself going out the
gate early in the morning like this had always flashed through
her mind at least once every morning for a very long time.

Lionfish

I WAS A promising standing researcher at an oceanography lab in a southern seaside town. Things having come to this, I'm not going to reveal the name of the town or the lab. I'd walked the same path for more than ten years in order to become a researcher. Until the incident, I never questioned myself, or had the slightest doubt that I would continue doing what I was doing for the rest of my life. The slightest doubt? Perhaps I did have some doubt, the slightest doubt. No occupation is completely independent of the secrets the world tries to hide, or the crimes, big and little, that everyone is partly involved in. In particular, when your field of research is the expansive field of edible ocean fish, directly related to nearly everyone's daily life, the world's temptations lurk in every corner.

When you're affiliated with a certain lab, you can't be unaware that the experiments you conduct could be used for something you detest. How many people can say with conviction that there wasn't a report they casually signed, or unclear results of experiments that had to be put to a stop with feelings of uneasiness, or falsified results which they unwittingly corroborated? How couldn't I have had any doubts as a mere researcher, and not, say, a project leader? When you're young, you rage and despair now and then. You turn on your boss, and publicly criticize him. But things like that don't happen often.

It's different when you're older. You see things differently, and if something isn't terrible enough to threaten all mankind, you might turn a blind eye to it. And something that dangerous would rarely, if ever, fall into my hands without some objections. Important decisions are made higher up. People in my position go to work for simple pleasures, such as the pleasure of confirming that one plus one is two. You tend to put aside little conflicts, imagining that the outcome of your experiment can improve human life to some degree. This idea always led to conflicts between Pink Anemone and me. Pink Anemone could never put conflicts aside, and doubts, big and small, tortured her day and night.

Even if there were minor conflicts, they were exceptionally rare and didn't make me think that I should leave the lab to do something else. I was a stuffy and timid young man who thought it was a tremendous step to change jobs or even just research areas from edible ocean fish to edible freshwater fish. Even when the director of research, who knew my quiet passion for deep sea fish such as fangtooth—which I called poisonous snake-tooth fish—lanternfish, and dragonfish, suggested that I go study abroad for a year or two, I only smiled wryly, saying that it was too late. It was just around that age that I decided to get married.

My real vocation, however, wasn't as a researcher in that lab, in that city. I had a dream too. I wanted to be a sculptor. I don't know if I had a good hand at drawing. Not a single teacher in the little fishing village had told me about my hidden gift or talent, so there was no room for illusion. I enjoyed making things when I was young, and I remember that I was the most ecstatic when I was making something with dirt, dough, or clay. I made everything I saw in the seaside town—people, friends, lobsters, starfish, coral, agar-agar, and even the countless fish in nets—with a lump of mud the size of an adult finger.

But I was born in a time when such things couldn't be enjoyed by a boy from a poor family. So one day, I decided to forget about my desire to draw and form worlds out of mud, the same way I forgot about the migraines or chronic gastritis that beset me at times, and I did forget. How many people don't harbor a secret dream like that? At any rate, the forgetting didn't get in the way of my living. Then the incident took place, as if to punish me for getting used to comfort and indifference.

The death of Pink Anemone had effects that lingered with me for a long time, long after the death had taken place. It's not something I like to think about. Her death kept pulling at me, as if there was no end to it, like a black hole, and then let go of me all of a sudden. Pink Anemone's brother, who at a young age had been studying abroad in China with three other kids, came running back, which wasn't a problem. But then he threatened to kill me. He had often joined Pink Anemone and me to go out for a drink, and was the only person from her family I'd met. The day before he left for China a couple of years earlier, Pink Anemone and her brother and I drank late into the night, having a good time. I could still recall an image of him carrying her on his back and disappearing into the car. He had been the picture of dependability, but now he was threatening to kill me. I think it was because I didn't know how to look sad enough to rip your heart to pieces. But he himself hadn't shown any sorrow, mostly due to his anger toward me.

The woman in her late fifties who became, however briefly, my mother-in-law, with crooked teeth and overly heavy makeup that marred her generally glamorous appearance, claimed that I had somehow aided in or encouraged Pink Anemone's death. She'd been unable to deal with the sense of injustice and sorrow at having lost her daughter because of a marriage she'd never approved of. I don't know much legal terminology. But the woman claimed that I intentionally made Pink Anemone ingest a fatal dose of alcohol, and abetted the death by just watching when I'd known she would walk into the sea and die. I have nothing to say about such slander. She might have been right on every point. Depending on how you saw it, I mean. What could I say, when we had drunk together, and I had seen her walk into the sea, even though I missed the moment when she sank underwater. I could only remain silent in the face of such insults, as I had no evidence to prove it otherwise.

Pink Anemone's father, however, takes the prize. He stepped right into misfortune and demanded an autopsy of his daughter's body. He was a hopeless judicial scrivener who believed only in what was visible in a time still rife with the invisible. That's when the pain I had to endure reached its climax. When I heard the news, I wept for the first time for Pink Anemone's death. I'd been her husband for only half a day, but my opinion mattered more than theirs, I thought, and even conveyed the thought to them once or twice. But the moment she died, I'd lost my right. Poor Pink Anemone, who had people like that as family. I realized only too late where her fastidious and stern way of dealing with people and herself had come from, as well as her demand for absolute and unconditional love, which had thrown me into confusion as to the kind of person she was. I was sad that I had come to realize this too late.

Fortunately, the doctor's opinion calmed Pink Anemone's father. The fitful attempt at an autopsy only served to reveal the little weakness that Pink Anemone had so wanted to deny, something I knew but hadn't divulged: the alcohol poisoning that had been quite far along. It wasn't the direct cause of death, but was serious enough to be fatal for the weakened heart of the deceased.

For Pink Anemone's family, the results were a bolt out of the blue. All the noise quieted down with that bolt. If not for that, I don't know how much more torment I would have had to endure. If I'd forgotten that people who experience death look for someone else to shift the misfortune onto, and that the person can't easily break free from the misfortune, I wouldn't have survived, being subject to all the whims of Pink Anemone's family.

I was thoroughly hurt, but I survived. And suddenly, I became endowed with a formidable power. Without knowing what that power was aimed at, I left the position I had worked a dozen or so years to obtain. It wasn't that I had any specific plans for what to do next, or feared the way people saw the tragic incident that had befallen me. The life I'd lived thus far, the life that hadn't presented any alternatives, seemed futile now.

My father was a fisherman. He had a little boat, weighing five tons at most, on which he caught fish in the sea near his home. With the passing of time, I've come to understand his sighs, his stubbornness. It was one night when I was a child, seven years old. My father, restless, heaved a deep sigh and got to his feet as I slowly dozed off to a misty world of sleep. He walked out the door, and across the small yard . . . and never came back. Not the next day, nor the day after. His little boat had disappeared somewhere, and he was found on the other side of the coast, with a strangely peaceful look on his face. In my memory, my father remains forever young, always leaving for the rough sea in the mist, again and again, never to return. Now that I think about it, the little boat I'd rested my feet on at the beach, where I spent my last hour with Pink Anemone, looked just like the boat my father had made himself. The peeling blue paint, the size, the shape, everything. Did I think about my father's boat on that beach? I did, but it was something that preceded thought.

I never thought about the boat. Just as you never stop to think about breathing as you go about your life. That's what all the boats in the world are like for me. Everyone is drawn to something despite himself. Perhaps I was drawn to all the little boats in the world despite myself. So I left my job, my home, and my friends. Like she who walked fearlessly into the misty sea, with a very violent storm coming, as if she were standing before a vast continent. I went toward my own little boat.

"I'm sorry, I'm really sorry," I mumbled to myself from time to time.

The words weren't only for Pink Anemone, who'd been my wife for one day. They were for everything I left behind, especially for my past self, whom I took apart in an instant.

People said that I was in shock at the death of Pink Anemone. That's why I left my job to go off someplace where no one knew me, they said. They were just saying, in a roundabout way, that I had gone nuts. And I knew that as soon as I turned around, they would say more blunt things, such as "He's crazy," or "He's far gone." They were right. I was quite far gone. I'd gone over the boundary. One day, I just turned into a vagabond, wandering aimlessly around the world. I took care of everything I had by giving it away or selling it. I condensed all the files that summed up my past onto a diskette, put it away in a safe deposit box in a bank, and took off. I left those who pitied me, laughed at me, raged at me, and at times loved me, far behind.

What I check at every step of the way, what makes my head grow cold and makes me shiver as I think about it, is the fact that my will is strong enough to disregard the pity and contempt with which the world looks at me. I know what strengthens me.

Leaving's not a simple thing for someone like me. You have to put your daily affairs in order with accuracy, speed, and organizational skill. Yet despite all the things I had to do, I found myself sitting about absentmindedly. In those moments, the woman I encountered under the sea filled my mind entirely.

Because of that image, I was able to leave with ease, to get my broken self up and be on my way again, on the path I'd set out on with that image in my mind.

At times, people I met on the road asked, What on earth did you see? They wanted me to tell them about it.

But I dare say that such requests were the most difficult for me. People think that encountering and then describing beauty is one of the most blissful things you can do in the world. There are so many things you can think of as beautiful. I, too, used to be someone who was easily moved by the slightest beauty. When I was working as a researcher, I took pleasure in talking for hours about the magical colors under the sea penetrated by clear sunlight, mostly to win the hearts of people I met at various gatherings. But somewhere along the line, I started feeling nothing but boredom as I made people marvel, talking with some exaggeration as well as expertise about the things you could touch by reaching your hand out, the festival of lights under the sea that was so beautiful that it would make even people who were afraid of the sea replace their fear with enchantment, with the help of some equipment. But I have no intention of denying even now, or ever, that the world under the sea, which had so captivated me, isn't beautiful.

What I'm trying to say is something else. There's a kind of beauty that cannot be described. Nothing throws you off more than having to talk about such beauty. But how unfortunate is someone who has never experienced the feeling of captivation that can't be expressed in words? These unfortunate people always asked me to explain beauty to them, because they didn't know that such beauty existed. There are people who know that the desire to talk about such things, and the impossibility of doing so, results in a fitful confusion as great as the captivation itself. They keep quiet without asking any questions. If the others ever trembled while seeing sublime beauty, as I or countless people in the world have, they wouldn't make such requests. They would probably say, "Beauty makes you open your mouth, and cry, and laugh. Beauty takes people's breath away, but at the same time, makes them go on living. Beauty makes people ill, but also heals them."

That's the kind of beauty I encountered. A woman that beautiful. For a moment. For one minute, at most. After that, most of my time was devoted to finding that woman again.

She Touched the Strings
of an Abandoned Instrument

SHE DIDN'T MAKE it far the first day.

And it seemed that it wasn't her aim to go forward, to go far. It was like a sort of inertia, and she would go away during the day and come back at night. This went on for the first several days.

She stood looking at the streets that were once familiar to her, but which now took on a different smell, color, and ambience in the rain. There aren't that many places you can go early in the morning, walking in the rain. It isn't because it's quiet, early in the morning. She knew vaguely that quiet times now belonged to a rare order that couldn't easily be found in the world. She went into a brightly lit convenience store, and stood drinking honey tea and looking at the street drenched in the rain. She looked with concern at the street, never at rest and never without noise, as if it were a river she had to cross. Her gaze rested for a while on a tramp, lying stretched out like a sore of the city, on a plastic seat at the bus stop under a lit streetlamp across the street, seeking refuge from the rain under the flimsy roof. She got another cup of honey tea. There was no voice saying,

"You're having two cups in a row!", nor any hand taking the cup away from her. Gradually, she would forget what she'd learned. She might forget, in a very short time, the information, habits, and knowledge that have piled up in her like dust without her even knowing.

She was deeply absorbed in the raindrops falling on the sidewalk, forming ripples on the surface beyond the glass wall. And when the raindrops stopped forming ripples, she went outside. The tramp on the seat across the street was gone. In the sky that was gradually turning blue, dark gray clouds rushed off somewhere in a group, as they do from time to time on early midsummer mornings. She thought, "When summer comes, I'm going to walk around in the rain wearing yellow rubber boots."

She made her way to the market, which was just coming alive. There, where plastic curtains were lifted, hoarse voices talked to each other, display stands were set up, and where the steam began to rise, she took a breath. Deeply, and then many times. As the plastic covers on the display stands were removed one by one, and glossy vegetables began to fill up the streets of the market, she found the scent she'd been looking for, the scent of a time gone by. Men in shabby clothes sat down at the stands and began to slurp soup. Men who looked like the tramp at the bus stop. She sat down at a stand set up by a woman who was stirring a pot of rice soup with a sleeping child on her knees. The child was sleeping peacefully, with a sad little frown, amid the commotion and the smell. Taking her time to chew the rice, she reached out her long, slender fingers, and touched, once or twice, the cheek of the sleeping child with dried snot under its nose and with blistered lips. As if to touch the strings of an abandoned instrument. As if to wake a child who wasn't there, as if dead.

Dazed, she walked around the streets of the market. Her mind became refreshingly clear as the lights came on, the noise grew louder, and more and more people filled the streets. She roamed around the streets lined with dry goods stores, butcher shops, and wholesale light fixture shops, and alleyways full of hardware shops.

A man moving a load yelled at her from a distance as she stood dazed, absorbed in the vague movements in the middle of the busily growing market.

"Move aside, girl. Why are you hanging around here when you should be in school?"

The words didn't apply to her, but she liked hearing them. There was someone who would say such words to her! She played around for a moment with the man's cart. When she came running out from among the shops and stands that were expanding as if ready to explode, the city was fully awake.

The daylight hours on the first day went by quickly. No one recognized her. She knew that there was an hour at which people would recognize her. And although she couldn't explain it to anyone, she knew how to go about it so that people wouldn't. She walked a lot, and ate a lot, on the first day. She went about here and there, like a chess piece, from the street stands and snack carts in the alleyways to the streets in the market. Gradually, she felt her body breathing pleasantly with simple, repetitive movements. She didn't go far. She always returned. It wasn't that she was afraid; it was more that she was waiting for the right hour to be ready for a long journey.

So on the first day, and the second, and the third, she always returned to the neighborhood when it grew dark, and stayed at a little hotel nearby. The hotel that had always been so brightly lit that it seemed you'd be able to look right into it when you looked at it from your rooftop. Places have a strange power, and when she returned to the neighborhood, she always thought of Shark, Starfish, Conch, and Agar-Agar, whom she'd forgotten about completely. None of them had ever complained about the hotel, which could be seen from the yard or the veranda if you just lifted your head a bit. Even when a man came out of a door on the top floor, probably of a private home, and looked down and spit while smoking, they didn't complain, as long as the spit didn't spatter onto their house, or fall on their heads. They had forgotten how to complain. She rented a room in that place. It was a small, smelly room with a balcony. Instead of a door that led out to the balcony, however, there was a window.

Through that window, she caught glimpses of pale-faced Shark doing his morning workout, honing his movements, and Agar-Agar leaving the house, her hair still unkempt, and Starfish, smoking out in the yard after everyone else had left. As always. She almost called out to them. She'd been without her voice for so long that she might have sounded like an animal barking, but in any case, she wasn't desperate enough to make whatever sound she could. She saw Agar-Agar returning from the market in the evening, carrying plastic bags in both hands, and Conch, dusting off her clothes and standing on tiptoes to look inside, then putting the key into the keyhole. The place, which she gazed down on in the morning or in the evening, looked peaceful and lonely and far away.

On one such day, when she returned to the area she'd left, she recalled a night long ago. Her memory of that night was floating around in a corner of her brain like a white buoy, with foam in the shape of a question mark lapping about but not moving onward. This memory became a part of her body and was too familiar to recall as a memory. Eventually the question mark got swept away on the water. She couldn't be swept away with it though, because the memory was still floating around like a buoy. And her voice didn't leak out of the buoy. That night that her memory now carried her back to, she realized that words were no longer necessary in the world, and so she forgot how to speak.

That was it. She lost her words because she came face to face with a world that required no words. It began as a feeling, as if a solid metal sheet were pressing down on her heart. The pain was in her heart, but the two hands that were causing the pain were on her neck. She opened her eyes, but couldn't see anything. What she remembered from that night was the touch of the hands taking turns, squeezing her neck. Her exceptionally long and slender neck bore it for a long time. Enough time for her to give up speaking. The nine-year-old girl swallowed up at once the labyrinthine time that told her words would be unnecessary in the world that was awaiting her. When her thoughts hovered around that time, what came rushing back was the deep compassion she felt for those to whom the hands belonged. Then the contours of her memory became less distinct to her. She rid herself completely of the memory of what had taken place that night, emerging from a blurry haze. The memory would never come back to her with clarity.

That autumn she left, a great rain poured down. And it drizzled throughout her stay at the hotel overlooking the house she'd lived in. Now she felt that she was ready to go someplace else. She boarded a train to the sea only because of the simple association of water with water. If it hadn't rained, she might have chosen another direction.

Starfish

THIS IS WHAT I think. If someone asked me, this is what I'd say. That I, we, have forgotten Jini, and that it didn't take long for us to forget.

I thought we'd all starve to death without Jini, but that didn't happen. Shark took even better care of our money and down payments, and clinched big and small contracts as if Jini would return soon, so he must have put aside quite a large sum of money. I thought it wouldn't be bad to live like that for some time, or for a long time. There's no chance that Shark didn't fore-see the possibility of Jini getting into an accident, or something unspeakable happening to her. He even talked to me about what we should do if something like that happened. Mostly, he told me about the state Jini was in before she left home. But Shark was much too worried and on edge. A contract was a contract. It would be ridiculous if no compensation was made when some-one was fatally wounded or killed. People's lives shouldn't be treated casually—the world was made for people to live in, after all. I know that once, when the car Jini was riding in bumped into the one in front of it, Shark received a lot of money for the shock, even though no one had been hurt, saying that Jini had suffered emotional shock, as if she were pregnant or something. Yeah, we learned that even without Jini, this household kept running, even better than before.

I gradually stopped getting up in the morning and busily calling here and there to ask about Jini. You could, of course, say that I got tired of it because there were no results, but to be honest, as time went on, I began to think vaguely that finding Jini might not be good for all of us. Imagine Jini coming back to live in this house when everyone was getting used to her absence and things were settling down. Picture yourself standing before Jini, who doesn't take her expressionless eyes off of you, as if she's looking right through you, without saying a word. You'll experience how her eyes bring out a mysterious sense of shame that's alive deep within you, that feeling of unease that comes over you when you've done something wrong. We've all felt as if we'd become butterflies or beetles pinned down before that gaze. It has a way of paralyzing you like that. You know the sweetness of oblivion, don't you? And that sometimes you have to forget in order to survive.

There were some people who said they'd seen Jini. About five or six of them called. They usually called when there was an article in the paper about Jini. I know these people well. The kind of people who are drawn like moths to a flame, I mean. You can tell by talking to them for a minute. They all come up with things that sound plausible, like that they're great fans of Jini, but the only reason they go through with calling our home is for the reward we'd pay if the information led us to Jini. I have no desire to talk on the phone with such people, or take action based on their reports. I don't know if Shark or Conch ever got calls like that, but I never even talked about them.

At any rate, the feeling that every day would be spent asking around or speculating about Jini, or waiting for her, and that things would go on that way, was a nasty one. But I didn't make my decision based on that feeling. One day, I just came to realize that I no longer wondered what Jini was doing or where she was.

How should I put it? It felt as if I'd put down a load I'd been carrying in my arms until they had ached, but it also put me in a vacuous state. That night, I drove all night on the highway. I felt somewhat better afterward.

It would be hypocritical of me to go on making a fuss about carrying out the ritual that took place in this house every morning. I'm not someone who has something I need to uphold to the point of hypocrisy. Besides, there aren't that many people in the world who can keep up their passion for a long time. Most people give up somewhere along the way. I'm just one of the countless people like that. For a while, waiting for Jini was a collective passion for the people in this house. But all things fade away with the passage of time. I think that's a great relief.

If everything in the world remained vivid forever, people would go crazy. If the flames of hatred for someone burned without end, if an orgasm lived on for years past its natural conclusion, if fear continued on every moment with the same intensity . . . Just thinking about things like that is a nightmare for me. All things take place in an appropriate timeframe. For too long, we lived through Jini, for Jini. Now it's time to forget her. I just hope that with the forgetting, our fear, too, will come to an end.

Yes, fortunately, that's how we survive. A crime that once turned the world upside down is forgotten, and another crime takes place. Life goes on that way. When you're surrounded by foul odors for a long time, clean air can give you a headache. I don't expect a lot out of life. I just want to live in peace, without incident, then disappear without a fuss.

I can't say that I feel at ease forgetting about Jini without going in search of her, or even making more active inquiries. I was the one who put a stop to the private investigation on Jini, commissioned by Shark. He'd agreed with me on the decision, but I'm not sure if we shared the same reason I had. Shark only said that Jini wasn't coming back. We had nothing else to do but go through the motions of looking for her. That was enough, he said.

Once or twice, I thought about where Jini might be and pictured myself getting ready to leave in search of her. But in the end, I decided not to. How could I leave the house and the family to go look for Jini, who could be anywhere? No one besides me could manage the household. Who else would have prepared three meals a day for the family, and who knew what could happen to Agar-Agar if I'd gone? Just imagine. Who in the world would have dusted and taken out the trash? Who would have made peace between Conch and Shark when they fought, opened the gate when the mailman came, or supervised the cleaning of the septic and the water tanks? Who, besides me, could give an appropriate answer when someone called about Jini?

There's also the issue of my feet, which keeps me from leaving. I'd use public transportation, of course, but you can only go so far in a vehicle. I'd have to walk a lot. Looking for someone requires being on your feet. But because of the chronic but hidden sores on my toes, which everyone otherwise compliments me for, my family, at least, knows that I can't go on a long walking trip. You wouldn't think something like that is important, but you don't know what it's like if you haven't experienced it. My toes, the only part of my body better than Jini's, made me suffer whenever I walked because of the hidden sores. Try to imagine how far you could go on toes like that. Would you want to ruin the one part of your body that people complimented you on? I couldn't. And I can't live for a single day away from this city. I detest mud and winged insects like moths. I loathe centipedes and worms. I don't know why, but I always think of things like that when I think about going off to look for Jini.

I have, of course, pictured myself going away carrying a little backpack, as if to go on a picnic. If it was a simple trip like that, I would've attempted it many times already. But why should I, of all people, do something like that? What about Agar-Agar? Or Conch? Or Shark? I get angry when I so much as think about it, as if I'm already underway and am suffering from insomnia because of noise from next door in a smelly inn. Why do people think that I should be the one to find Jini? What people call common sense is so unreasonable. They're saying I should sacrifice once again, since I am Jini's older sister and have always sacrificed little things for her.

But I can't. Looking for someone requires knowing them well. Little clues that would give you a general direction are very important. She's my younger sister, but I don't know Jini very well. I can make three or four lists of her likes and dislikes and so on, but do I really know what she likes and doesn't like? It feels as if all my memory has vanished. I never knew a lot about her in the first place, but now my mind has gone blank, so no, I can't do it. It would be ridiculous for me to go look for her, because I am much too ignorant about her. I'd soon lose my way and losing one's way is a terrible thing.

Above all, I have no reason to go look for Jini. Even if something has happened to her, it would be too late for anyone to do anything about it by the time I found her. That something . . . It's too abstract for me to understand, but everyone lives and dies once. So going off now with nothing but vague feelings of anxiety would be reckless. I'm sure nothing's happened to Jini. Nothing can happen to her. I have a feeling. The same kind of feeling, almost a certain knowledge, that something unfortunate would happen to me as soon as I left this city.

So I can't leave the city and go wandering around the peninsula in search of Jini. I'm not the one who left. I'm not, we're not the ones who have forgotten Jini. Jini has forgotten us.

I went out to the river a few days ago. It's where Jini used to ask Conch to take her. The water at the riverside was black. If you bent your head and took a whiff, you might smell something foul. The image of Jini's face floated up to the dark surface of the river like a cause for anxiety, and I erased it from my mind immediately. I can see why the family of someone who has died of a terminal illness would want to go on a trip somewhere as soon as the funeral is over. Now I'm going to open my eyes in the morning with a clear head, think about the fun things I will do that day, light my cigarette, smoke without regret, and roam the city without worrying that Jini might appear from out of nowhere. I'm going to meet decent people. While I spend time with them, the wheel of life will go on turning without a hitch. When my body grows ugly and my expression and skin grow old, I'm going to bid the world farewell without delay. There's no reason to hesitate, or run from it.

Lionfish

I INVESTED MOST of my severance pay in a medium-sized four-wheel drive I bought and renovated. I spent nearly a month in bringing to realization, to a degree at least, the dream I'd shared so often with Pink Anemone. I couldn't really say that I decided to carry out this plan, which certainly wasn't a simple plan, to honor her memory. To be honest, it was only when my brother-in-law came to make peace with me before returning to China that I remembered that I'd often talked to Pink Anemone about this little dream.

"I'm sorry, I'm really sorry." I said these words over and over again to Pink Anemone, who'd died before she ever got to join me on the journey we'd dreamt about.

"We'll buy a Jeep with a powerful motor that can run on steep mountain paths, rough rocky paths, and even snow-covered roads. And we'll renovate the interior into a room that moves. Oh, there are caravans, of course, but they're too big and bulky, and don't drive as well. You can't go on an adventure full of surprises in those. You can only drive through boring flatland or dull mountain paths. Soon enough we'll find the latest high-tech, high-performance Jeep. The moving room I have in mind is different from a caravan. Let's put a folding bed in the back seat, and a minibar as well. And all our diving equipment, of course.

We shouldn't forget a heater that works whether or not the car's ignition is on. We'll stock the minibar with strong drinks, and we'll drive day and night. We'll stop when we want to stop, sleep when we want to sleep, drink when we want to drink, and when we want to make love, we'll just park the car in the woods or on the beach, and draw the curtains . . ."

Listening to my excited voice, Pink Anemone would get drunk in advance. The car I bought, of course, wasn't quite the one I'd pictured, and the renovation process was more complicated than I'd imagined, and required a lot of time and money. But what hit me the day I came back with the car, newly remodeled into a sort of little room with the necessary accessories, was a severe sense of emptiness. I didn't know where I should go with the car, made with such care for a long distance trip. All I could do was drive around aimlessly like a loser on the road in the middle of the city, full of busy, aggressive traffic, trying to decide on a general direction. But I didn't even know if I should really go somewhere.

It was on one of those aimless days that I came to know the identity of my little goddess—that's what I called the woman I saw under the sea on that fated day. As with most of the other things that had happened to me until then, it came about through a difficult and complicated process. All I knew about her was that she'd been on an underwater shoot for a summer product to be launched by a major company, which would still take a long time to come out. It was vague information for someone like me, who didn't know anything about such things. Those tidbits of information, which had come out of the mouth of a waiter working at a coffee shop in a hotel in Seogwipo, became embedded in my mind.

I tried to gather information on my little goddess in any way possible. But I'd never pictured in detail how I would actu-

ally meet her or what I would do after meeting her. I couldn't
imagine myself finding out her number and calling her, going
to where she lived in order to meet her, or waiting around for
her to come outside. Nor could I picture the kind of house,
neighborhood, or alleyway she would live in.

What if the place I had go, driving an unnecessarily large
car, with all kinds of flashy equipment, was an apartment in a
little alleyway that wasn't even five kilometers away? Whatever
I tried to imagine, it didn't seem right. But with the same blind
diligence that used to come over me when I worked at the lab,
I devoted myself to gathering information on my little goddess.
As if that was my goal in life.

The public relations department of the company in question, however, didn't take me seriously, as if to say that they'd
dealt with enough people like me, off their rocker, and wouldn't
offer me much information, treating me like a hunting dog set
loose by a competitor. They seemed to be saying that there were
people everywhere smitten by advertising models. But going
around trying to gather information wasn't an entirely useless
endeavor, even though I was treated like dirt. I found out the
name of the agency that was in charge of the ad in an article
pinned to a bulletin board that hung on a corridor wall of the
public relations department.

The advertising agency looked at me with even greater suspicion. Through them, I learned that my little goddess went
by the name "Jini." It had been quite a while since I got rid of
my computer, which in the past I couldn't go without even for
a day. I went to an Internet cafe in a corner of the city, and for
two nights I looked up information on my little goddess named
Jini. But when I saw a picture of Jini on the screen for the first
time, I was rather untouched. What I saw in the pictures on
the screen seemed to have nothing to do the little goddess

I'd encountered under the sea. The images of her face were just like the countless faces of women on television who all looked more or less alike. I even suspected that I was looking up someone completely different, based on the wrong information. But fortunately, the vivid image of the little goddess, enveloped in the blue water of the sea, rose to my mind, blurring the image on the screen.

Even now, I can't really say exactly what it is that I want. I've asked myself from time to time if I really want to meet the little goddess. But I've never had a clear answer to that question. Once or twice, I've felt afraid, picturing her coming toward me, and running.

What I do know for sure is that it isn't my intent to gather all possible information, especially secret information, on the little goddess. I've been disappointed enough by the countless articles without any substance. There was no end to the information, but what was helpful to me could be summed up in just a line or two. I wrote that information down on the first page of my travel diary:

"Jini is the stage name of the little goddess. Age 17. She lives with her family, consisting of three people besides herself and has been out of touch since last September. Possible causes include accident, disappearance, or kidnapping for ransom."

There was only one thing that made my heart skip a beat, and that was the fact that the little goddess disappeared not many days after I saw her for the first time. I couldn't help thinking about the mysterious and telepathic exchange between us. It was a groundless delusion. Based on the circumstances that day, every second of which I could recall vividly, it wasn't likely that she'd seen me, and even if she had, I never thought that I had any power over the life of a little goddess.

Paying visits to various agencies, I had a chance to see how people who fall in love become obsessed. There, people who wouldn't have left any impression on me had I met them elsewhere were behaving in unusual ways, overcome by a passion, persistence, and suspicion that overcame them only in those places. When I knocked on the door of the fifth agency I visited, I sensed, in the look that the staff gave me, that I could have been taken for one of them. But everything happens as if by chance. That day, I met someone there who led me, whether prepared or not, a crucial step closer to the little goddess.

She Boarded a Train to the Sea

SHE WATCHED THE autumn rain dampen all that was dry, without stopping, without making noise. She knew that not all of the wetted things would revive. The scenery, still gray, filled her view. Cold cement buildings flashed by in the wet fog, as if about to melt away, as if floating. She read the signs on buildings large and small, rows and rows of vague codes. There wasn't enough time to read them all. The names of buildings and shops were cut off in the middle. Her gaze rested on a middle-aged man hunkering down and smoking a cigarette in front of a shabby building, fitting right into the background as if he'd picked it with care; then a group of men looking up at the sky, hands in their pockets, drawing or erasing something on the ground with idle feet now and then; then a crowd of youth standing on a street corner, restless with pent-up anger; then moved on to other things. When you reach the end of a city, another city begins, and uneventful events take place outside the train window. Morning hours on an O-train are ill-suited for embarking on a meaningful adventure.

Only after the train had been running for a good while through the repetitious scenery in the fog and autumn rain did she realize that it was a local train that stopped at almost all the stops. She had taken the train because it was immediately

available when she arrived at the station intending to go somewhere, but if she'd known that it was a local train, she would
probably have taken it more deliberately. She didn't know which
direction it was headed, but she knew that to get to the sea, no
matter where you went, you had to get off the train and walk
some distance. She had seen quite a few landscapes, quite a few
people, and quite a few countries, but she had never yet seen a
train that took you right up to a beach. She was ready to walk a
lot, and for a long time.

Not too many passengers were on the train. People don't like
the smell of wet iron, and the low speed of a local train makes
them anxious. Several men, with the threatening look found on
the faces of people who are ready to push and shove each other,
raised their heads which had been buried deep in their seats,
looked quickly around, and then lowered them again.

It's a mystery how she could travel on in this way without
being noticed; a wonder that people didn't notice her beauty,
which became even more remarkable without her makeup and
wardrobe. It must be stated, however, that she didn't make any
effort to avert her gaze or conceal herself. It's possible that in the
process of returning to a state she had nearly forgotten about,
everything from her expression and gait, to her gestures and
complexion, had begun to change little by little.

And little by little she began to forget or lose the set of rules
for training her body, those regarding sleeping, eating, resting,
walking, even breathing, which she had learned over a long
period. One by one, she abandoned the countless rules devised
to control her body. She slept until intense rays of the sun came
pouring in through the window of a one-night lodging, free of
fear and anxiety for the first time in a long time, and on some
days, she greeted the evening with no memory of what she'd
done all day in the room. She opened her eyes when she felt

like it, and lay down or walked or sat as her fancy struck. She would trip and fall while running to feel her heart beating, or fearlessly climb a rough and empty mountain path, unafraid of any changes that might come over her body.

Rules of the body, of course, acquired over years, are not forgotten at once. It was true, for instance, that she needed some time to free herself from the old, obsessive notion that she had to breathe out while putting her left foot forward. For the first time in a while she ate without restriction, and welcomed without suspicion the ecstatic feeling that came over her when swallowing something raw. Used to a diet of steamed vegetables or boiled meat or fish, her stomach did put up some resistance, but before long her body adjusted to the new practice. Strange that none of the things that people around her had feared took place. Her body didn't change in an unseemly way, her skin didn't grow coarse, nor did her hair grow rough, and she didn't show any symptoms of obesity, such as shortness of breath. Still, she hoped that some kind of change would occur, something that would signal a new life.

As the train advanced from station to station, she realized that there were no longer boundaries between cities. When she could no longer distinguish between the greenery connecting one city to another, or the colors, shapes, and lines that are bound to exist between cities, she doubted for a moment if she would ever reach a seashore, a seashore she'd always thought she would visit on her own someday, even if she didn't currently have a fixed destination. When the scenery showed no signs of change, remaining the same one station after another, she wondered for a moment if the train wasn't a toy train that always ran the same course over and over again. But at each station, one or two people got off, and another one or two got on.

She didn't really want to see anything in particular at the beach. She just wanted to descend, peacefully and indifferently, into the sea without purpose as she had once done. She had closed her eyes to give herself, without any fear, to the warm, soft water. She remembered the day well. It was a part of her photo album, one that was hers and hers alone, something that made her happy whenever she pictured it, like the image of the boy with rolled up trousers walking into the woods while playing music.

You could say that she had, since that day, been preparing little by little for a trip. The day of the underwater shoot was no different from other such days. On the yacht, people talked loudly and shouted with impatience as always, what with all the unnecessary fuss, anxiety over possible accidents, and missing equipment, of which there was always at least one piece. For several days now, she'd been repeatedly practicing going underwater for the shoot. What she remembered, though, was the single descent, the boundless sense of relief in her body from the temperature, color, and feel of the water. You could probably say that the moment she entered the sea, as if entering the belly of Agar-Agar, with a near-perfect faith, her plans for a trip had already come to a head. When she opened her eyes, only the realm of the sea, light blue and transparent, existed before her.

When she opened her eyes, an old woman was sitting across from her. Her cheeks were hollow, and her eyes dim and sunken. She began to move her lips as if she'd been waiting for her to open her eyes. The old woman's voice was barely making its way up her throat, and she had to stare intently at her lips.

"I feel like I've seen you somewhere. I've met so many people that I can't tell who's who anymore. Anyway, this train goes to that city, S, right?" said the old woman.

The train was not headed to the small city in question. She shook her head no. Since leaving home, she'd felt the urge to talk many times, but never acted on it, afraid that only the sound of wind, or that of an animal, would come out of her throat.

"I seem to have lost my way again. I guess I got on the wrong train on top of that. I've forgotten where I live, who I am. My son must be looking for me. I'd appreciate it if you could take me to him. You can do that, can't you? I think you will. When you're as old as I am, you get a sense about these things," the old woman said, and handed her a grimy piece of paper.

On the piece of paper were the old woman's name, resident registration number, and address. The area was on the outskirts of the city she had left. She had no destination she had to reach that day, so she nodded at the old woman. The sea would still be there tomorrow, and the day after that.

"I knew it. Thank you. We need to get off at the next station. My son must be so anxious for me to come home," said the old woman.

The old woman clutched at her as they walked down the train steps at the station, and she wouldn't let go even when they got on a train back to the city, and as they wandered around a mazelike alleyway in the neighborhood, looking for the address written on the paper. The old woman wasn't of any help in finding the house. When she reached the address that was on the paper, evening had fallen, and the old woman who'd been clutching her arm had disappeared. A young woman came out of the house and told her that no old woman by that name lived at that address; that several girls around her age had already been there at the request of an old woman. She walked through the alleyway many times, but could find no trace of the old woman.

She had left in the morning and already the time had grown late. She made her way toward the center of the city, a place of countless round tombs of flickering light. At last she reached the middle of the desert of lights and walked and walked. She might have ended up walking all night, until she reached a station, where trains that were to depart from this desert of lights sat clustered together.

Conch

I SEARCHED AND searched for clues that would tell me where Jini might have gone. I thought endlessly about the reasons she might have left. What had happened that I didn't know about, that I wasn't involved in? I always sensed something sinister in this house, a feeling that I was being shut out. Had Jini met someone I didn't know about? Had someone made an important proposal that I wasn't to find out? I checked, again and again, her belongings, her room, the places she frequented, which I remembered vividly. But I found no clue, no reason that could make me understand. People in my area of work have suggested that it's time I started looking for another job; that there were plenty of young people like Jini, and plenty who could be even bigger than she was. I have, in fact, met many young people who were recommended to me. But I know that it's all meaningless unless someone brings me Jini right now.

You can be sure that those who have worked with Jini will feel something akin to the sense of loss I've been dealing with since she disappeared. I'm not surprised that the fallout from her disappearance is so intense, as the moments I spent working with her brimmed with joy that was almost addictive. I don't know where she got her ability to understand what I meant, and create the feeling I was aiming for, with a simple expression or gesture. When all the feelings a product can conjure up—joy, sorrow, gentleness, bleakness—emerged through her body, something unforgettable took place. I remember her every gesture, every expression that made those watching stop their thoughts to follow her movement. And at the end of her movement the name of a car running through a desert would appear. Through Jini, things are born and given a names! Then there's the profile of a woman in unfathomable grief. I have never watched that scene for more than ten seconds without tearing up. Jini had the ability to obliterate the cameras surrounding her, the people moving busily about, the machines, in order to take us to the heart of a story. Who wouldn't want to call her when they saw the expression on her face? I always thought it unjust that what people remembered through that face was nothing but the logo of a telecommunications company.

I often felt that some fiendish power took over when she was in front of the camera. There must be quite a few people who don't like her for that reason. I understand how they feel, as there were moments when I felt frightened, looking at Jini who'd become unrecognizable in an instant. Without Jini here now, I have the courage to face the question that comes over me at times: Was it through an ability that neither Jini nor I understood that she created the astonishing images that penetrated deep into people's minds? In an instant she would express something that went against everyone's expectations, and that, in the end, was what was chosen. When I sensed that a power even Jini herself didn't understand had taken possession of her, I felt ecstasy and fear at the same time.

And I had a feeling that the quiet, strange girl might take me to a faraway place, a place that was beyond my reach.

I have considered leaving Jini, many times, in very specific ways. But I never stayed away from her for more than three days. Once, as if to flee from her, I left with a friend from home who had come to see me for the first time in a while. But Jini found out somehow, and came down to where we were staying in a provincial city. There in the small yard, she took my hand in hers, and shaking her head slowly, she wrote on my palm, "Don't run, Conch."

Jini never said, though, that she would wait for me, or that I should come back. That's how she is. Having said what she said, she got back in the car she'd come in, and took off without looking back. How could I not go back? I had abandoned everything and left with a man, a childhood friend from home, for the sole reason that he wanted me. There were a couple more instances like that. When Jini didn't come looking for me, I didn't last long. That's how it was. On the very first day we met, she took my life in a direction I hadn't anticipated.

How often I had dreamed of going someplace far away with Jini. Our work trips without Shark or Starfish were always a party. But when others pushed their way in between us, everything grew stale. As if playing a little game, Jini and I would pack a small suitcase for the trip we would take someday. We would pack even the very little things. We were prepared to leave at any time, but we never got to go anywhere, just the two of us, other than for work. And then she left without me, while I was preoccupied with other things.

At moments, Jini would write on my palm something that was frighteningly relevant. And when she did, I couldn't defy what she said, as if I'd received a message from an oracle. Jini's messages were always brief. It wasn't necessarily because she wrote them on my palm, I knew. And how simple were her words: Laugh, Conch. Forget, Conch. Listen, Conch. I knew what difficulty Jini was having. No one else knew that with time, her hearing was growing weaker and weaker. But in the face of my concern, she wrote on my palm: "It's okay." I can see everything.

Poor Jini. Poor, poor Jini.

In the house bereft of Jini, something smells rotten. The smell pervades every corner of the house, as if rats and other animals, trapped in the roof, have begun to die and reek. There's no one, however, with the time or courage to tear up the roof and see what's there. Everyone, like me, is going about their business outside the house, so as to stay away from the smell.

With me, it's different. I leave the house because I can't just stop and stay put. Stopping, for me, is death. So as I endure the unsettling days of storm, I go around to the offices of acquaintances looking for someone like Jini. I stare at the people passing through, with an unstable, empty gaze like that of someone looking for someone to seduce.

I ran into the man while doing just that, going haphazardly around advertising companies looking for traces of Jini. First I heard a man's voice, calm and determined. The voice was asking the clerk at the information desk a question. I distinctly heard him say "Jini." I'd been sitting in a guest chair, observing, as I was wont to do, the countless people roaming the place, and almost cried out. I managed to calm my heart, which had begun to thump at the sound of her name, and approached him and studied his profile to see if he was someone I knew. The tanned, strapping young man, wearing a thick fur coat and hiking boots, too early for the season, was asking the clerk for Jini's contact info. I'd never seen him before. The clerk, who knew me well, shrugged her shoulders with an uncertain look on her face, and looked at me as if to ask what I thought. The man followed her gaze and turned toward me. Our eyes met. In the eyes of this stranger, I saw something very familiar: the sorrow of someone searching doggedly for something they can't find, someone suffering from a sense of emptiness.

Shark

I GET UP every morning and lift weights. I turn into a raging animal fighting against a weight pushing down on me, and lift lumps of iron as if lifting a chunk of mountain I'm about to hurl away, or the Earth itself. As I struggle against the weight with all the strength I have, with my eyes closed, I fall into a sort of vacuous state in which I let go of my consciousness. I must be addicted to this state. My life is very regular and restrained. I have learned countless sports since growing up—all kinds of ball games, boxing and wrestling, taekwondo and judo. But early on, I gave up on sports that required you to team up with anyone else. I'm a solitary athlete who trains himself. I give myself a task each day, as if training an animal: myself. Weightlifting, boxing, javelin, or knife throwing suits me. I have no teacher. I've had no training from anyone. I learned everything on my own. I've never gone without at least one or two hours of physical workout in a day. And I've never violated this principle, even when I was having a terrible day and had to put everything else on hold. I decided one day on these hours of physical training for no particular reason. I probably got into the habit of working out while struggling against my hatred for the world that took hold of me abruptly.

I was born with weak health, but no pathogen can enter any layer of my muscles now. I overcame the morbid shyness of my childhood in the same way. Only those who suffer shyness know how painful it is to stand face to face with a stranger, as if facing a dead end, despite all the cares you took so as to not put yourself in that situation. No one knows of the hours of pain I endured to learn how to stare, with a straight face, at the empty spot between the eyebrows and not into the eyes of another person.

There is no mystery in the world, no secret to it. The world has become generous to those who destroy, shout, and oppress. I put my best efforts into learning how to destroy successfully, shout effectively, and home in on a vital spot when making an attack.

Defying what you were born with—there's no greater defiance than to defy yourself. I put great time and effort into making myself over—my nerves, my muscles, my temper, my constitution—as if replacing parts in an enormous machine I wasn't satisfied with. I never take in more than a fixed amount of calories, and I never utter anything unnecessary. I don't talk to people I don't like, and I don't reply when they talk to me.

By focusing, I can remain for hours as if dead, my eyes closed, having removed from my mind all the images that harass me. If there's one good thing about myself, it's my body. My body is my religion. I believe nothing but what the body says. My bones are solid, and my muscles are tough and stubborn. My nerves respond to everything in an indifferent, almost mechanically violent way, unless it's something quite extraordinary. But when I have figured out who it is I must attack, who it is I must destroy, my body does not back down an inch. I detect the malice of the world around me through my own ampullae of Lorenzini, a bioelectric sense that sharks possess, and I've developed an extremely persistent disposition through the resistance and perseverance I was born with. I don't respond to just anyone at any time. I close my eyes to the malice of the world, its twisted games, until the time is right. Responding at the exact right time doesn't have to mean responding to the external world. My reaction can show through, of course, through a cold smile or violent behavior. But in most cases, I leave the place and head someplace else before my body reacts in any way.

Early on, I learned to see through people who were ultimately indifferent to anything other than crying out me, me, me; those who felt strongly for nothing but themselves and their own misfortune, wallowing in self-pity, like bugs trapped in a narrow, filthy waterway; those who were obsessed with themselves, lamenting whatever it was they lacked, interrupting people and saying, "As for myself . . ." and "I'm like that, too," before anyone even asked. They come up to you with a benevolent smile on their face, a smile so sweet that it melts your heart, as if they loved you, and then stab you in the back with a knife. The world is full of bodies that think of nothing but getting a chunk of your flesh, even at the height of pleasure when they're crying out that they love you.

The world I see hasn't always been this dark and suffocating. I assume that even for me, there was a time of genuine, warm smiles. But if such a time did exist, it didn't last long. That's for sure. The few faded photos I still have clearly show the contrast. In the three or four black-and-white photos I'm glaring at something with a frown on my face. Even when I'm sleeping, I don't look at peace. An unhappy boy with tender skin, three, four, or five years old at most. The boy's fists are clenched, and his eyes shut tight, as if he knows that the most difficult struggle in the world is the struggle for a bit of peace for the soul.

No. The boy in the photo has never been at peace since. I learned early on that it was meaningless to try to talk to the world, and to respond seriously to what it said. The tender skin soon grew rough, like the skin of a shark, covered in teeth, and the boy wouldn't have hesitated to feed on its own eggs for survival. I learned this, and I never had any real experience to overthrow the knowledge so it became the only thing that sustained me.

The boy in the faded photo, torn up and discarded, is the last I remember of him. To be honest, I have no memory of myself from before the photo was taken, or after. So the ten years between the ages five and fifteen might as well have not existed for me. I must've gone to school just as other kids did, of course, wearing a uniform, and I must've caused some problems just as they did. I might have been somewhat odd, being awake when others were asleep, and asleep when they were awake. I do recall myself on very rare occasions, scrambling out of a dog hole behind the school along with other kids, smoking a cigarette, which I liked neither the smell nor the taste of, in the stinking back corner of the bathroom, getting beaten up in a dark basement by a group of kids I didn't know, strangling someone with a nasty smile on my face, punching my own cheeks with my fists while crying, and growing more and more violent. But it all feels unfamiliar, strange to me. I have no witness, no proof telling me that those images are really of me. What in the world was I doing? I don't remember what specific experiences I had growing up that made me become who I am now.

Who ever said oblivion is something to be ashamed of? There's nothing so comforting as oblivion. I have no desire whatever to bring back the lost time. Not only that, I lock up most of what's happening in my private life at the moment in a box of oblivion, let it suffocate, then annihilate it. Doing business with people who don't know the joy of annihilation feels so outdated.

There was a time when people whispered behind my back, a long time ago, "He must've been wounded badly."

Okay. Let's say that it's true. But it's not something that should be spoken of in the past tense. Every moment inflicts wounds. I'm not the kind of person who sits there licking them. No one can say that the disorder, chaos, and immorality brought on by oblivion are greater offenses than the disorder, chaos, immorality, and corruption of those who remember all and commemorate the past. I'm of the mind that it's better to destroy everything and begin anew than it is to fix and mend. That's what revolution means to me. People who seem completely different from each other, and two opinions that seem at extreme odds, can be brought to a dramatic reconciliation. That is my kind of revolution. But I'm a revolutionary who requires no followers, heroes, or victims. I am constantly in search of the most sure and convincing way, the way and the time to overturn the world that has taught me defiance, contempt, despair, disappointment. I know that an idea like that doesn't come overnight, but my body twitches with impatience at times. At least I put my oblivion and revolution into action at every moment. Alone. With my entire body.

The world, I dare say, is quite accommodating toward my plans in a way. The world falls, breaks, declines, and retreats, as if to make way for my plans. The world is rife with wars, and as relentless desires flood the world, people grow simpler and poorer, and finally disappear. We would have to come up with a different name for people of a world like that. I wait, bored, for the world to collapse on its own, like an eroded mound after a monsoon.

I play a game while I wait. Making a deal, for me, is a game that brings me great pleasure. When I'm making a deal, I am persistent, just as I am in the dead hours of the game, giving it all I've got. I'm Shark, I say in introduction, and let the other know that I'm ruthless when it comes to making a deal. Ever since I began to handle work for Jini, her value has doubled, maybe more. I make propositions, but I never push or beg. I examine only the essence and explain only the essence. The price I suggest for each part of Jini's body is absolute. And intolerably low, according to my measure of value. Watching Jini, who radiated more and more brightly each day, I wasn't sure what price I should suggest in the future. The silent light emanating from her draws out the truth from deep within myself, a truth about to become extinguished. The contour of her chin, the movement of her body at a certain moment, the angle of her gaze . . . I know when these things emit the most intense light, so I can demand what I demand. The light radiates for a moment, then vanishes. I enjoy making deals for this vanishing light that's consumed in a moment. The price I demand for each transaction, more than twice the usual price, is nothing compared to the light Jini radiates each moment. That price is the greatest gift I can toss to shortsighted people who have no ability to recognize what's before them, to see the truth.

That Jini exists, at least, the one human being I acknowledge and accept, will be a small comfort to me to the end of my days. But will it really? The opposite might be true. The moment I'm comforted, my own self is denied. Humans have always had two conflicting desires: the desire to be comforted, and the desire to betray and destroy the one who's comforted you, for the sole reason that they brought you comfort. These two desires, in the end, are like two sides of a coin.

Jini isn't absolutely necessary for the pleasure that comes from making a deal. A deal is a deal, after all. In this world, there are countless people who come up with highly advanced rules to enjoy playing games. Look at all the brightly lit buildings that light up the night. The countless buildings filling up the earth are packed with people who enjoy playing simple games of business transaction. Unless a fundamental change comes about, these games will continue and intensify and take over the world, its days and its nights. Unless they've already come to an end. I'm one of those people who refer to themselves as "I," even though they know there's no innate "I" anywhere in the world. Nothing is unique: not my desert island, my method of death, my pleasures and despairs, oblivion and annihilation. Still, I am I.

Her Body Language Became a Dance

NO ONE KNOWS how she freed herself from the circuit of the train and got back on her way. What she'd thought was the circuit of the train might have been nothing but a feeling created by the fear that gripped her before she left the city where she was born and raised, where her family was. She could have stayed in the circuit of love out of habit, as the habitual chain of love is often a closed circuit. Then one day, she was finally ready. She stood at the open door of a train that had come to a stop, pulling the blue suitcase that had accompanied her since the day she left home, carrying a little pink backpack on her back, and wearing a fluttering gray dress that looked too flimsy for the weather. She stood there for a little while, as if waiting for a scheduled procedure.

If someone had taken notice of her as she stepped down from the train that stopped for a moment in the empty station, they would have fallen at her two little feet, encased in muddy sneakers. That day, her beauty had reached its peak. And some peaks endure, like her beauty. There was no one at the station after the train left, save for the stationmaster who came out for a moment, ducking his head in the chilly weather, and communicated with the train operator by raising a red flag to signal the time of departure. Only a few flowers, out of season and withering from sorrow, it seemed, were to be found in the station yard.

Having arrived at this station, she performed a brief dance that could make you think that she'd become aware of her fate for the first time. It's possible, of course, that no one considered it a dance. She got off at the station, stood in front of the long, outstretched railroad tracks, and lifted her hands horizontally. She looked around, smiling a smile that would be on the lips of a goddess who took pity on the world, if such a goddess existed. Looking at the steel railroad tracks, the rocks, the weeds, the station made of bricks and cement, the sky, the electric wires drawing a parallel without meeting, the mounds of dirt in the yard, she turned, as if in reaction to the gravitational pull of her two raised arms. When she returned to her original spot, the smile was gone from her face, but her face, sober now to a point beyond recognition, shone forth more brightly than ever.

Her face shone because of a certain sense of anticipation—a quiet excitement for something incredible that was about to happen. On top of that, she was at the resort city she had passed through on many occasions. Without traveling far, she had come to a city that was close to the sea. But after just several days of travel, the sea was no longer something she felt she must see. Her desires changed nearly every day, every moment in this way, so often that she didn't even remember what desire had possessed her just a moment before. Sometimes a strange sensation came over her, and then she could bring it back whenever she wished. She could become the sea when she closed her eyes, and sometimes, she became a mountain even if she didn't yearn for it. If she told anyone this, they'd say that she was losing it. Fortunately, she felt no need to tell anyone this, nor could she. She had momentarily hoped that her voice would return, but it had gone its way, never to come back.

She moved forward, driven by these unfixed desires. She came
out of the station and headed to the little square. In summer,
the station bustled with people on holiday, but in that season, at
that time, there were only three young people, dressed in shabby
traveling clothes, at the little square. The two boys and a girl,
who seemed to be around her age, followed her with their eyes,
their faces expressionless, as she appeared in the empty square.
Their blank faces smelled of something burnt. It was as if a part
of them had been burnt by a passion that couldn't be borne at
their young age. The young girl put down her dirty old backpack
on the ground, and not taking her eyes off of the young woman,
came toward her. The girl reached out her hand. On her palm,
creased with dark lines, were little carved ornaments in the shape
of animals, and she thrust them at her.

"Want to buy some of these? We're traveling but we're out of
money, and we've been starving since this morning. I have other
stuff over there. Come with me, I'll show you," the girl said.

The girl, who dragged the young woman over to her friends,
took out a box from her backpack and opened it. It was full
of roughly carved, fingernail-sized wooden ornaments, in the
shapes of a bird, a bear, a cow, a snake, a frog, an owl, and so
on, which could hardly be distinguished from one another, and
earthen carvings of triangular shapes with comb patterns, and
carvings with indecipherable patterns that resembled bird prints.
The tired, indifferent looks on the faces of the boys turned gradually into looks of curiosity, as if they were wondering which
animal she would choose, or as if she would buy something from
them, unlike the others. She took the box the girl handed to her,
felt the objects carefully with her thin fingers, and at last, picked
a triangular carving with geometric patterns. The girl quickly put
a string through the loop and hung the carving around her neck.

She swept back her long, thick hair, which came down below
her shoulders, and showed the ornament to them, then stood

still with her eyes closed. She leaned to the side and shut her eyes tighter, as if to detect something that was happening within her body, as if to focus her mind so as to convey something she wanted to express in the best way possible, or as if fumbling through the scenes that rose from deep in the recesses of her mind. Then she began to move. Her movements should be called simple dance movements, similar to the dance she'd performed at the train station. She turned slightly as she lifted her arms, one higher than the other, then lowered them. What else could this be but a dance movement?

Before these young people, she expressed herself for the first time through body language. Only she knew what she meant by raising her hands slightly, then keeping one in the air and putting the other behind her, and lowering them slowly in a spiral motion. It seemed as if she were expressing gratitude, or trying to communicate a very specific message. Each of the three seemed to understand the movement in a different way. In any case, they responded to her dance, as if a thin veil that had been drawn over their eyes in the form of drowsiness or boredom had been lifted. Three different responses and expressions arose, each quite distinct.

"You want to stay with us? Sure, the others will be fine with that, too."

"Okay, but first we need to go warm ourselves and get something to eat. Then we can get to know each other."

"You know people like us? So you want to help us."

In any case, the three, who'd been watching her perform a dance that wasn't a dance, gathered their things as if bewitched, and went after her without a word. They left the square in front of the station and shared a dinner at a place in a little alley. They were busy filling themselves up and didn't talk much, but she learned that C, the girl, and P, one of the boys, were a couple,

and that E, the other boy, was their longtime friend. They didn't
ask her many questions. C did ask her one or two, hinting that
she knew who she was, but none of them showed further interest, as if such things didn't matter to them. Likewise, she wasn't
curious as to how the three of them had come to set out together,
where they were headed, and for what. Even if a bit of curiosity
did arise in her, it wasn't sufficient to be expressed through her
body language.

She stayed many days with them in the empty resort city. E
knew of a vacant summer house near a pine forest on a beach
that wasn't far from the city, and the three were trying to earn
the fare to get there. They took a bus, and walked a long way to
the beach. Even after they arrived, they had to walk for a good
while along the beach before finally arriving at a row of summer
houses that looked similar to each other. The wooden houses
were all empty, as E had said they'd be. He strode toward one
of them, pulled out the nails on the wooden beam on the door
with ease, then opened the door and went inside. He seemed
quite experienced. During their stay on the beach, they lived in
that house. C and P stayed in the one bedroom; E let her have
the couch, and slept on the floor. She felt like a ship that had at
last dropped anchor in a harbor she liked. She felt that she could
make a sound like a boat horn if she made a little effort, but her
voice remained stuck in her throat.

Staying with them in the house, she watched E and C take
a small, sharp knife in hand in the evening and make wooden
carvings of cows, bears, frogs, owls, and birds, and the next day,
she began to make carvings, too, of simple animals. It felt quite
natural to her. As people are prone to feel when they're tired,
when she sat with them in silence, carving wood, she felt as if
she had, long before she was born, carved animals out of wood
somewhere else as she was doing here now.

It couldn't be just any animal. The same animals, and the same geometric patterns, had to be carved in wood. She didn't question it. She did learn through their conversation, however, that E was the one who had first suggested it, and that the family he'd left behind had a long tradition of carving wood for a living. She liked to carve bears and birds. They carved in silence, and E and she were always the last ones to stay with it. As they worked, they heard C and P making love in the bedroom. She made ornaments in the shapes of frogs, owls, and snakes, so absorbed in her work that she got blisters on her fingers.

On the day after, they went to a market in a nearby town, or a place where people gathered, and went up to them and sold the carvings as C had done with her. She, too, sold her wooden carvings, of course. When people asked the price, she spread out five fingers and shook them twice. People, depending on what they made of the gesture, gave her five hundred won, a thousand won, or sometimes, five thousand won. After selling the carvings, they each put the money in the leather pouch they carried around, not checking to see how many each had sold, and for how much. She reaped the biggest harvest, but her friends paid no particular interest, as if to say it was just beginner's luck. They could all reach inside the pouch for the money to buy what they needed, and paid for what they all needed with the money. But the money from the ornaments sold was never enough to supply all their basic needs.

None of them worried about the next day, and the couple of young lovers seemed carefree, as long as they could make love every night. One late night, no different from any other, she saw E looking quite depressed, unlike on other nights, as he listened to the sound of C and P making love in the bedroom. E had told her one day about the taut triangle between the three, the reason why they were driven to wander around as they did. E

loved C, and could not leave either C or P even though C had
chosen P, his best friend from childhood. E had come up with
and suggested this way of life because he loved C, and P was
the friend who understood him best; and they had accepted
his suggestion.

She lifted E's face and tilted it toward herself, and whispered
to him in body language so beautiful that it would probably
make him tremble for a long time to come. She sat with her arms
behind her head, and bent her body forward and backward in
an infinitely gentle motion; through this brief movement, she
conveyed her message to E.

"Let me comfort you, E. Teach me how to make love. Then
you'll be set free."

E came toward her as if drawn by irresistible power. She
spread out her arms as widely as possible, and embraced E's firm
yet tender body. She had never made love before, and sat still
waiting, just holding him so tight that her face turned red, not
knowing what to do next. Without looking away once, E made
the seeds of joy, dormant inside her, come to life, as if teaching
her how to forget the loneliness, pain, and fatigue of the body.
In an instant, she felt the fabric confining her tear open. She no
longer needed E's guidance. She let her body dance, as if whispering infinitely comforting words to E. Their bodies danced
to a single rhythm, until all events and all memories burned to
white ashes amid the simplest and deepest ecstasy, and soared
far away into the universe.

When she awoke from a deep sleep the next morning, she
sensed that E had left on his own, having broken the balance of
the triangle he had too long maintained with his friends. On the
faces of C and P, she saw both the sadness and the sense of free-
dom that come over you when you lose something valuable you
had to carry with you for a long time. They would now go in the

opposite direction from E. She gave them the blue suitcase she'd
been carrying around. She gave it to them because E had taken
the pouch of ornaments, but she no longer needed it anyway, as
she'd spent most of the bills that had filled up the suitcase when
she had first set out. She could travel more lightly now.

They left a letter for the unknown owner of the house.

"We apologize that we forced open the door and spent many
days in your home without permission. We apologize further for
having burned the books, paintings, frames, photographs, and
anything else we could, to endure extremely cold nights."

Thus they left the house they'd stayed in for many days and
arrived at the fork leading to the market of the beach resort city.
There she said goodbye to them. With a bewildered look on
their faces at the sudden imbalance of things, they disappeared
off toward a crowded street corner. They seemed to be searching
on the street for their friend who'd left from the way they looked
around. They looked forlorn, but after just a few steps forward,
they began to walk with the careless lilt of youth in love. She was
headed toward the beach, then turned around.

She stayed around the beach for one or two more weeks. She
met a good number of people. There were some she didn't want
to part with, and with some, she experienced deep, intense love,
but because it was deep, and because it was intense, it didn't turn
into anything more than a sort of image, a vague impression that
stayed with her. A part of her may have hoped that E would
return, as she had. But he didn't, although she wandered around
for many days near the empty summer house in which they'd
stayed. One moonless night, she danced for herself alone on the
sandy beach. Looking at the sky, she arched her body like a bow
and said to herself, "It's not you I'm waiting for."

Agar-Agar

"MAY THERE BE comfort for all pained souls born into this world. May there be peace for all who are pained in body, pained in mind, or pained both in body and mind, suffering unconsciously, mocked and cast out by family, betrayed by friends, rejected by neighbors, born in misfortune, living in loneliness, having no forgiveness, working and toiling, weeping and wailing, suffocating with sorrow, abandoned and brokenhearted, neglected by parents, and racked with heartache.

"The sun will rise and dry all tears; the shadow will cool the wounded, burning heart; the night will come to bring comfort and rest to the unhappy souls in the world; you'll open your eyes to see the sunny hills, the green trees, the high sky in peaceful silence; difficult times will pass, and a time for laughter will come; your love will be taken for what it is, and so will your words and endeavors and integrity, without confusion or misunderstanding. You will rise high and look down with pity and compassion on all who fight and push and shove. . . ."

The woman poured out these words in rapid succession, but she wasn't satisfied. Her words lacked something, but she felt frustrated, not knowing what was lacking. She had a hard time focusing her mind today. Her voice cracked and her mind was scattered, and she spoke halfheartedly at times. For nearly thirty-nine hours now, she'd been sitting on a rock, waiting for something substantial to gather inside her. That something, however, which formed around the eyes, then filled the mind and lightened the body, would not come to her, no matter how long she waited. She knew that a more powerful flame kept that something from gathering drop by drop.

At the top of her voice and with all of her heart, she called out the countless names of gods floating around in her mind, which came to her on the wings of the mountain wind from the valleys where people cried out in desperation as she climbed the mountain. Still, she wasn't satisfied. As soon as she stopped, the rambling, restless flame filled her body.

For that reason, her eyes blazed as she looked at the clouds approaching from a distance—as if the clouds were her enemy, an omen of misfortune that must be dispelled. She had no choice but to postpone her descent, as the familiar flame that had begun to grow inside her several days before wouldn't be subdued, not even with all the names she poured forth. She had been on the mountain for nearly two weeks now.

This time while climbing she'd never said a word to the others who were there. She felt that the ominous flame that had taken hold of her would come spilling out as words if she opened her mouth. She couldn't say a word, not when she woke up early in the morning and washed her face in a stream, or when she ate, or when she went into the tent in the evening to shelter herself from the cold. When she came across a familiar face, she would turn around brusquely. She was afraid. Yet she was the only one who'd asked the drink vendor, who came up all the way to the peak, not to forget the rice wine that would warm the bodies of everyone on the mountain.

She didn't weep and wail as she prayed, either, as she usually did. She was tired. She hadn't stopped eating and drinking, and the cold wasn't unbearable yet. But she felt so worn out that she asked herself if it wouldn't be better not to go down at all if she couldn't come back up. She was aware that moments often came upon her when she wanted to let it all go, as if she'd lived to be more than a hundred.

She felt at times that she was about to die. She had no control over herself, and the flame she thought had died out kept coming back to life and burning her. Once it returned, it followed her, without giving her so much as the time to question why it had. It was always that way. She vaguely sensed that the time to extinguish the flame at last was near, and she trembled at times out of fear, and at times, impatience. Sometimes she came out of the tent and spent the night huddled in the cold, afraid that those around her would notice her spasm. But far from feeling cold on those early winter nights, when the temperature dropped below zero, she couldn't sleep for thirst and fever. Her body grew more feverish by the day.

She knew full well what this flame was that had seized her like a whirlwind many times before. But this time, she felt uncertain. She felt that she no longer had the power to subdue it, and sensed in rare moments of clarity that she was doomed to give herself over to it.

She shut her eyes tight and shifted her focus, trying, in an effort to appease the flame, to recall moments of simple joy that the target of this flame must have once brought her. Sometimes, the images brought about the opposite effect, fanning the flame, so she took care to creep furtively into a dusty corner of a drawer hidden away in the recesses of her mind. She stood on her tiptoe, and quietly entered the room where she'd lain alone in the dusk, clutching her swollen belly.

She vividly recalled the pulse of the pain that pierced her internal organs at regular intervals, and the urgency of calling someone for help had been so great that even now, after such a long time had passed, it made her loose flesh tighten and break out in goose bumps. Outside the dark room, her daughter, who had just turned two and had a short life to live, was playing on the ground; the sound of her playing was swallowed up in a violent wave of pain that shot through her body, after which she passed out. She didn't even hear the cry of the newborn baby, which was supposed to have been so boisterous that it made all the neighbors gather even from a distance.

As she shut her eyes tight and searched for traces of joy that would quell the flame that engulfed her, what filled her mind was the distinct feel of rough skin, bumpy as a toad's back, that had once covered the newborn baby and was prickly and abhorrent to the touch. She had hit her head against the wall many a times, failing to understand her relationship to this child which had gone wrong from the beginning.

It wasn't that she had found no joy in him. But the memory of the joy that had come from the body of a small human being, who had clenched his tiny fists and cried, and smiled, and sucked on her breasts, was much too faint to subdue the ominous flame that seized her. She'd wondered so much about what had gone wrong and where, without coming to any conclusions, that she no longer cared to find the answer, or even to be genuinely concerned with it. The auditory pleasure the child brought when he began to talk lasted briefly, and then every word that came out of his mouth appalled her; and his good looks, which everyone stopped to compliment her on, only became another reason for uneasiness as his paleness and sharp features began to combine in a diabolical way.

"It's no use!" she cried out, as if heaving a sigh and coughing up blood. As expected, her effort to grasp at memories of joy, which rarely ever came, then vanished away, only awakened in her a deeper gloom and melancholy. These then quickly turned into heated rage, without any transition in between.

"Oh, it hurts, it's killing me!" she shrieked again. She kept picturing specific scenes, and when she did, her breathing grew hard and she clenched her teeth, trying to bear the unbearable. In those scenes, which manifested themselves in different ways, someone was trying to kill her youngest daughter, and when she tried to get a look at the person's face, it invariably turned out to be the face of her son, the child who had made her pass out twenty-two years ago. Pale with fright, she stared at the images whirring through her mind, as if enduring the dark night ten years ago when she had lain still, unable to move, even though she knew whose hands were strangling her daughter, simply for the pleasure of destroying something beautiful and tender, the pleasure of being cruel to something weak.

"I was so ignorant!" This time, she let out a long scream. She was right. She was young and immature, and was more afraid of rumors ruining her son's future than of her daughter being smothered to death. Whenever she recalled that suffocating moment, that moment alone without what came before or after, the face of her daughter would turn into her son's at times, and the face of her son, into her own. But the acts her son committed, faster and more intense than the rumors surrounding them, would never stop.

She sprang to her feet. Then she sank back down. When she was on her feet, she looked as if she were about to run straight down from the mountaintop. As she kept springing to her feet and sinking back down, people on the mountain gathered around her one by one.

"Hey, you alright?"

Instantly, she returned to cold reality. She sat back down on the rock, looking modest and proper. She gently swept back her unruly, disheveled hair, and waving her hand, said brusquely, "Of course I'm alright. Don't you have anything better to do? Go worry about yourselves!"

Something else she couldn't understand was why she always said what she didn't mean; it was as if there was something inside her, interfering with what she was doing. The thing must feed on the flame that seized her. In any case, no matter how well she meant, what she said didn't sound so nice, and there was nothing she could do about it. And she never added empty words to undo the damage.

When everyone scattered back to their spots, she clasped her hands helplessly and, swaying in every direction, began to send her despairing message to the countless brothers and sisters who communicated through the sky on the mountaintops around the world.

"A long, long time ago, a long time after this land had risen, there was a great big hand that looked like a bear paw, but was a human hand. It was the hand of an old woman who had borne a dozen children, and was so old that you couldn't tell if the hand was a man's or a woman's. There was no work in the world that the hand hadn't done. It had brought water, prepared food, raised children, sold things, weeded fields and paddies, gathered firewood, threshed rice, made kimchi and sauces, kept some from falling, picked up some who had fallen, beat the wicked, patted the good on the back, but what this hand was best at was soothing pain, pain in the mind, in the kidneys, in the gall bladder, in the small intestine, in the large intestine, in the heart, in all the internal organs . . ."

She raised her thick, stumpy hand and shook it toward the sky, and pressing it down around her heart, drew circles with it over and over again, as if to bore a hole into her chest. As she went on talking about the hand that looked like a bear paw, peace found its way back into her voice.

Starfish

GUESS WHAT I did. I've discovered something incredible. People always find out too late what's incredible. That's what so often makes life so bitter, but there's no need to despair. You know how many sayings there are that go something like, "It's never too late to start," or, "The thief who learns his trade late doesn't see the day dawning in his fervor." There's truth in all these sayings, or they wouldn't have come up with them.

It's a bit embarrassing to say, but what I've discovered is the simple fact that I could be dazzling, just beautiful. It happened by chance. I swear. I was staring at myself in the mirror one day, at the expression on my face, my smile, the curves of my breasts and my waist, and my buttocks and my shoulders, and for a brief moment, I wanted my own flesh and bones, skin and hair, parted lips and wet genitals. What turned me on the most was the seductive look on my face. It was only for a moment, but it was intense, and a little scary. Because I was looking at myself the way I looked at Jini sometimes, completely oblivious of myself.

I said it happened by chance because all human affairs have a higher chance of happening either too early or too late than planned, than vice versa. Anyway, this is how it happened. I was home alone, like on the day before, and the day before that. I wasn't staying home, of course, to take phone calls from people who said things like, I saw Jini sleeping in a chair out on the street, or, I saw Jini, looking exhausted and wandering around the outskirts of a city, or, I lived with Jini on a beach.

In my own way, I was making an effort to come up with a way to say goodbye to Jini. No one helped me. As usual. No one trusts me. What did help me was all the material on Jini that Conch had so carefully collected. Conch is one amazing woman. Looking at the material, I saw once again that someone like Conch and I would always remain apart like parallel lines, never to be brought together. I hate people who are so persistent, and so serious. But I was blown away by all the material. "You're amazing, Conch!" I exclaimed with exaggeration one evening when Shark was there. I'd always been stingy with compliments for Conch, but I felt bad for her—she'd lost her place after Jini disappeared, and she couldn't leave, either. But when I did, she looked at me as if she could see right through me, then went into her room. What should I say, that was the real beginning of my farewell to Jini. You could say that the look of suspicion she gave me gave me a sort of inspiration. Thinking back now, I might have been throwing her bait without realizing it. Telling her, I'm here, too, Conch; I could be someone you invest in, too, with so much passion.

At first, I was just going to take a look at the material Conch had collected, as if watching reruns of a popular TV series. I mean, it was just sitting there in a corner. Shark and I decided to clean out Jini's room, which became my job. Agar-Agar didn't care either way, but Conch was adamantly against it. She had no leverage, though. She was mooching off us, and she had no work coming in.

I thought I'd just skim through the videos, but watching Jini, who appeared scene after scene and tape after tape, I began to feel a little strange. I felt uncomfortable somehow. "Oh, I see now why everyone wants Jini," I mumbled to myself over and over. But the clearer the screen portraying Jini, the more certain I felt that she was dead. Sometimes I spent half the day fixed in front of the screen that displayed image after image of Jini. It was on one of those days that I said goodbye to Jini.

I did feel, to a small degree, the sadness and pain most people supposedly feel in saying goodbye. Yet something quite unexpected happened. I paused the video at a scene capturing Jini at her most radiant, and I sobbed and sobbed. I wept, shaking all over with intense sorrow, as if I'd witnessed the scene of an accident where Jini's beautiful head had been crushed, or where she'd been found in a hole dug under a spooky bush, or as if someone had brought me Jini's drowned corpse, swollen and unidentifiable. The sorrow, momentary though it was, was genuine. It was probably the first time in my life that such profound sorrow had come over me. It probably won't happen again. I refuse to let sorrow in. So this outpouring of sorrow, which reeked of mold from the old materials, was my way of paying respects to Jini's death.

After that, I began to stay home by myself and watch videos of Jini, mimicking her gestures, expressions, walk, and smile. I'm not so stupid, of course, as to think that I could be her. I know my body inside out. Stupid people and people who like to suck up to you say now and then: "How alike they are! I know they're sisters, but they're the spitting image of each other!" I've never once believed things like that. I always sneered at how superficial these people were. I know myself, how different I am from Jini. But I feel somewhat different now.

Before I begin my ceremony with Jini's videos, I take a long, elaborate bath. I put some pink salt harvested only from a desert, which Jini brought back from a country she visited for a shoot, into the bathwater that's just the right temperature, and then I wait for the bathroom to steam up. I let out a long breath, as if purging myself of all the impurities clinging to my body, and dip myself slowly into the water. My body becomes so sensitive that I can feel the minute processes inside my body, which is like a tube being cleansed. I gently scrub myself using Jini's sponge, pressing it against my skin so that the salt particles will soak into my body. I try lying still with my eyes closed, but there's nothing more difficult and boring than that. There's nothing I need or want to think about in that position. "Oh, I'm so bored!" I end up exclaiming, in spite of myself.

So as soon as I come out of the tub, I light a cigarette and start smoking. And that's just what I did that day. It was when I'd lit a cigarette and was standing naked in front of the mirror, without a thought of drying myself, that it happened. Was it the thin layer of steam covering the mirror? I couldn't take my eyes off the nude body of the woman in the mirror. What was pulling me toward itself with such great force was nothing other than the reflection of my own body. Oh, did I tell you that I decided to grow my hair? I can't report every little detail, you know. Anyway, this is what I saw: the freshness of wet hair that came down to the shoulders; the suggestive charm of the woman in the mirror, with a cigarette in her mouth and a slight twist of her waist; hazy, dreamy eyes, above all, bewitched by a female body; lips, slightly swollen from the water, parted to exhale smoke; and concealed genitals of the woman in the mirror, opening up like a flower blossoming in secret underneath the pubic hair, with drops of water like morning dew still clinging to it.

When I touched my breasts, the woman in the mirror touched her breasts. When the woman in the mirror pinched her nipple, my own nipple hurt. When I put my cigarette between two fingers and caressed the curve of the woman's waist with my other fingers, it was my own body that sensed the heat of the cigarette along the curve of the waist. But how unfamiliar to me was the woman in the mirror who had me riveted before her, and who was now staring at me as if bewitched. What I saw in the woman in the mirror was none other than Jini. Jini, who was dead. I was frightened at first, but dead bodies and ghosts, I learned, weren't so scary after all. You could say that I began to enjoy saying goodbye to Jini every day, growing more and more distant from her. Getting used to her death day by day.

Part Three

What made her start dancing?
Was there, inside her body, something that couldn't be put into words, making her dance?

Did some kind of ecstasy only she could feel turn her movements, so simple, into dance?

People who saw her dance for the first time couldn't help but ask these questions.

She Gladly Became a Reflection

HER FACE WAS now brown, and her body shone with a simple, healthy beauty. The only ornament she wore was a necklace, from which hung the earthenware charm she'd bought from C, with a pattern of inverted triangles, and a wooden bear she'd carved herself. She often walked barefoot, moving along the beach. She had no purpose, no plans. On one beach she saw a huge shark that had been dragged to the shore after attacking a fishing boat and injuring a fisherman. Lookers-on said that the sprawling fish was over three meters in length. Although the shark was dead, the crowd of people stood in the distance, and the deep, blue-black eyes of the shark looked colder now, making it look as if it would attack them any time. She'd never seen a shark before, and her gaze lasted longer on the cold eyes of the shark than on its frighteningly sharp teeth. Occasionally when she arrived at a dock and there was a boat headed to a nearby island, she got on the boat and spent half the day on a little island whose name was unfamiliar to her.

If there's a moment in people's lives when their body and mind are in bloom, at their most beautiful, you could say that she was in that moment in her life. Age seemed irrelevant to the moment, contrary to what people commonly thought, and for some who are blessed, the moment may last all their life, in different forms. She was yet too young to be in full bloom in every way, and her beauty, it seemed, wouldn't fade with time. Her body and mind had become strong through long travel and rest, deep sleep, and the experience of love. No fear could shake her up, and no threat made her cower. She cast away and lost much as she moved forward. She dismissed from her mind all the dark, fearful, painful, unjust, and sad memories that stirred up terrible feelings in her, so terrible that they made her wonder if she should give up on traveling and go back, fight them to the bitter end. Now that she'd rid herself of her past, no one saw in her 'Jini the model' who had once appeared on television or electronic displays in cities, or in newspaper and magazine ads, and who was considered a genius at transforming herself, now mysterious, now diabolic, and now a pale beauty.

When people did approach her in the evening, in cities she passed through, they would say things like, "Hey, I'll help you get a job at a nice place. Come with me," or "Come have a drink with me, little girl. I'll pay you plenty in return."

She smiled without malice at these men and women. They rarely persisted when she smiled at them that way.

She was sitting on the beach one day, watching the sunset. She'd just gotten off a fishing boat that had given her a ride. The boat had been rented for an offshore exploration by a group of college students studying oceanography in a big city nearby. On the boat, she had filled herself with the ark clams and other fresh shellfish they'd caught to kill time, so it was the perfect time to enjoy the grandeur of the twilight on an early winter sea, which formed into an enormous castle of red, violet, and slate-gray. The students had said, "Hey quiet girl, if you want another ride tomorrow, just come back here. We'll let you on."

She wouldn't be there tomorrow. There was nothing more that she wanted. She knew she had to be on her way again. A sort of intuition told her when she should leave after she'd been in a city or a region for a while. Sometimes it was a certain sense of danger approaching, and sometimes it was a feeling in people's eyes when they looked at her.

When the sound of children playing faded away, and the fishermen gathered their nets before the tide rose and left, the beach suddenly revealed its desolate vastness. Only a white dog remained on the sandy beach far away, following a smell. The sun and the sky, the clouds and the air, seemed to be creating a final spectacle just for her before the light disappeared as she sat on the darkening beach.

If there was one thing she had learned while traveling, it was that no encounter, no scenery, and no spectacle came to her more than once. Even if something similar seemed to happen again the next day, she knew that it was infinitely different from what had happened the day before. If she wept for a moment before the day's sunset, it was from nostalgia for everything that appears once, then disappears. It was as if she began longing for something even before it had vanished. Before setting out, she stood to express gratitude to the spectacle presented to her by the sky. As she grew more accustomed to traveling, she realized that the sea, and the things that surrounded it, inspired her body language in the most profound way. She danced with the joy and fulfillment that came over her like a whirlwind. She danced, repeating two movements, as if she herself were the whirlwind. Her upper body would twirl like a morning glory, then her arms would sway quietly and slowly above her head. In this way she expressed her gratitude to the world in twilight.

"Thank you, thank you, for showing me beauty. I'm sorry, so sorry, that I'm not as beautiful as you are yet."

As her body twirled and twirled on its own, she felt as if she would have no regrets, even if her life came to an end then and there. She closed her eyes as she danced, like someone paying her last respects to life—as she always did when she danced.

Her strength left her at last, and she stood still to catch her breath. She felt something warm touch her calf. Startled, she opened her eyes. There was someone lying face down at her feet, stroking her calf. Looking at the lumpy body of the woman, no longer young, she thought of Agar-Agar. But the woman's hair, done up in a knot, looked elegant. The woman, shaking her shoulders as she lay there, was mumbling something. No one had been there a moment ago, but now the woman was with her and a dog was circling around them.

Had she been more flustered, she might have said to the woman, "Try to stand up." But nothing but a rough wind came leaking out of her throat. She shook her head slowly, and took the woman by the shoulders and helped her to her feet. The woman, who would once have been considered a beauty, and was wearing heavy makeup, stared intently at her. Looking into the woman's eyes, which seemed to possess everything but her soul, she thought, you can't run from eyes like these, but she wasn't afraid of anyone anymore. The woman stroked her face with her hands and burst into tears. The coldness of the jewels and metals on the woman's fingers made little goose bumps rise on her neck, in the chill of the darkening beach.

"My dear daughter, I knew it. I knew you'd come back. That's why I've been coming here every day at this hour," the woman said.

She neither turned nor backed away, just let the woman do as she did. While traveling, she'd met many people who took her for someone else. They spoke to her or followed her, seeing in her a lover, a sister, a lost daughter or granddaughter. They came up to her, looked into her face, touched her from time to time as this woman did, and stayed with her for some hours, but with her remaining silent, they eventually turned away and left. She didn't know what it was about her that made them take her for someone else. She herself often saw Agar-Agar in many middle-aged women with a wide back, messy gray hair, a slow, often crooked walk, and somewhat distracted movements. What made these people see their sisters, daughters, lovers in her? She felt she could be whoever they wanted her to be, if only she knew. She hadn't looked at herself in a mirror for a long time and was gradually forgetting what she looked like. When she closed her eyes to picture herself at times, she could see only the ocean, mountains, high rises, the sky, a little room, animals or clouds, or a field of wildflowers, images that were a part of her.

Looking uncertain, the woman took a small step back from her. She knew how profound the longing for someone could be when you realized your mistake, so she'd learned to smile, to ease the transition from one moment to the next. Her smile, however, only drove the woman to greater delusion.

"Yes, of course you're my girl. You were always the prettiest when you smiled," she said.

The short woman barely managed to put her arm around her shoulder, and then walked with her toward a car parked near the beach. A middle-aged man who looked as if he'd given up on everything got out of the driver's seat and came toward them. The white dog that had followed them jumped into the back seat as soon as the door opened, and settled down in what seemed to be its spot. She hadn't been able to shake off the woman's arm because the woman was trembling. And now she was standing before the car, her head bowed as if she had done something wrong, because she wasn't the one the woman had been waiting for.

"Please forgive us, miss. My wife . . . as you can see . . . is unwell. We'd be so obliged if you could spare us some time," the man said, sounding embarrassed, but earnest in his desire to invite her.

The old man with white hair on the sides of his head bowed to her, who was so young. He looked tired from lack of sleep, as people who live with family who move between reality and illusion often do. But the reason she decided to get in the car with them, perhaps, had more to do with the dog, which barked at her once, looking more desperate than the man, and curled up to make room for her on the seat.

As always, she had no business to attend to that night, no place she had to be. She feigned barking in reply to the dog and sat down next to it. The dog, mistaking her for someone else, too, perhaps, rubbed its nose against her knees in a warm, friendly way. The woman seemed to have fallen asleep from sudden exhaustion, and the man looked relieved that the situation, which had probably repeated itself often, never to be prevented, had been resolved in a relatively easy manner. The car began to move along the dry path lined by pine trees, with the dust rising in the wind.

Lionfish

I NAMED MY car Icarus. I'm not sure why this car—with its three long antennae, which looked as if they had been installed for communication with a planet far from Earth, a silver its gray exterior, and an interior painted in black and gold for a comfortable yet sturdy feel—brought that name to my mind. I don't know much about ancient myths, but I suppose I felt that the name Icarus fit my car, which didn't perform as well as I'd expected. I was still happy, though, as my dreams for a mobile home, which fully met basic daily requirements, had finally been realized. Naming it Icarus, perhaps I wanted to assure myself that I wouldn't be so reckless as to fly toward the sun with waxen wings. At times, trying to establish objective distance from myself, I wondered if the mobile home I'd dreamed of wasn't, in the end, like the waxen wings of Icarus for me. How trivial and small are the desires that are fulfilled in our fleeting lives, compared to the dreams we might have had. We all know, however, that even the fulfillment of those few desires can rarely be called complete.

Conch. She called herself Conch. I was ready to open up to this woman, who, as we divers often do, had nicknamed herself after a sea organism. In the beginning, anyway. I didn't ask her anything further, since she obviously didn't want to reveal her

identity. Mindful of my manners, I told her my name, pronouncing each syllable clearly as if challenging her a little. But
as we talked, I couldn't help but withdraw the good feelings I'd
had. I came to think that if the woman, who seemed to glare at
me with a cold smile on her lips, hadn't uttered the name of my
little goddess, I wouldn't have gone with her to a coffee shop, led
by her decisive steps, let alone taken the trouble of spending so
much time with her. And yet, drawn irresistibly into her story, I
forgot about the unpleasant feelings I got from her.

Certain names make mysterious things happen. For Conch
and me, 'Jini' was that name. Little by little, the name began to
dispel the hostility I sensed from this woman, this stranger. At
times, I tried to understand her, even going so far as to imagine
that it must be the loss of the little goddess that had made her
so bitter. The fact that we'd been at the same place, at the same
time, brought us together rapidly, though we were so different
that we likely wouldn't have met even under any other circumstances. After confirming that we'd both been on the southern
island before our chance encounter, before you could even call it
a coincidence, Conch and I became obsessed with reconstruct-
ing what happened that day, down to the minute, down to the
second, almost.

"That's right, another little boat arrived on the island around
that time. You must've been on that boat," I said.

"Are you talking about the five-ton fishing boat? With three
red stripes on the side? That boat was carrying the camera crew
and the equipment. Jini and I arrived after that, on a white
clipper," Conch said.

"Oh, you did. We were busy getting ready to dive. And on
top of that . . ."

"When we were almost ready to shoot, some divers began to
go underwater, so you must've been one of them!"

Checking each other's memory like this was quite encouraging, and exciting, for someone like me, who'd been reliving the overwhelming memory of that day over and over again by myself. The excitement made me dream a foolish dream, feel as if I could rewrite my history after what happened that day. I would have met the little goddess on the island, my wedding the next day would have been postponed, and I would have said goodbye to Pink Anemone in a different way . . . Retracing memories of her own, Conch became consumed in this game of memories. But she'd been out of the water, and I in the water. What happened out of the water was always dull, compared with what happened in the water.

I pulled myself out of the game and fell silent. To talk about that day, I had no choice but to talk about Pink Anemone, in whatever way. But the reason I had stopped talking wasn't because of what had happened with Pink Anemone, which I had to disclose. It was the feeling that had come over me from the beginning concerning my little goddess, the sad feeling that there would be no good way to describe what I'd seen.

"A little goddess, wearing a thin, transparent blue suit, came down to me under the sea, curled up like a fetus in the mother's womb, swaying in the water, eyes peacefully closed."

That was the summary I'd taken more than a month to draw up for myself, close to what happened that day, though not very polished. But that wasn't exactly it, either. I rewrote it many times, but the sentence failed to express even one-tenth of what I'd perceived and experienced. So in the end, I avoided talking about it.

Confirming in our first conversation that Conch and I had been somewhere on the island together on the day before Pink Anemone's and my wedding, when the diving party was held, was a very important step in our relationship. Even though it was I who had seen the little goddess underwater, Conch knew so well about the very point I had difficulty expressing in words, and understood what I was trying to say without my pathetic effort to explain it in detail. Conch told me that she experienced something similar when she first saw Jini. Rare is the happy coincidence when two strangers sit down and talk face to face and recall at the same time, in almost the same detail, the color of the ocean at a certain hour, the smell of the water at a certain moment, and the subtle ambience of a moment created by the sun and the wind and the waves.

That's why I showed Conch Icarus that day. I did it almost on a whim. At first, Conch seemed to think that Icarus was just an ordinary car decorated by someone with an unusual hobby. Difficult as it was, I tried to tell Conch, as briefly and drily as possible, about how I had come to get Icarus ready since that day on the island where we met without meeting. Conch, who had been looking cool and aloof, as if she knew everything there was to know about Jini, showed some emotion for the first time. Icarus somehow proved that the change wrought in my life by a single encounter with the little goddess was more profound and complete than the change in her own life, even if she'd spent nearly ten years with Jini. This must have come as quite a shock. But the moment of shock didn't last. She carefully examined Icarus, asking one or two questions while looking as stern as a judge, then at last gave a meaningful smile. It was the smile of a chess player thinking she's finally found a match.

What I like about my relationship with Conch is that there's no need for guile or deception. Without any qualms, she was looking for her Jini, and I for my little goddess; and we had confirmed in each other's eyes that we desperately needed each other to do so. What we could do to help each other had become clear. But although Conch and I had come to a tacit agreement,

I wasn't sure yet as to why I had to find the little goddess. If I had to say something in explanation, I could think of no other reason than that I wanted to witness what I'd seen underwater once more, just once more. I trusted that the moment I met her again, the reason I searched for the little goddess would be made clear.

What Conch told me about the whereabouts of the little goddess, or in other words, how little she knew about her whereabouts, led us to the conclusion that Conch and I should set out in search of Jini without delay. But how? There was no need to plan. First, we simply needed to get in the car and go where Conch's intuition led. An order of rank had somehow established itself between Conch and me, and I was following her will and silent command. What had given rise to this order of rank was Conch's ability to talk about my little goddess. She had quite a lot to say about her. What could I do but be quiet, listen, and follow? No matter how permanently engraved the image that had captivated me was, I couldn't talk to Conch about that brief moment, which lasted less than a minute, over and over again.

The decision to share the small space in Icarus with a woman I'd never met before, not just for one day but indefinitely, didn't come easy. All I knew about the woman, besides that she'd taken care of Jini for a long time, and that she was, in her own words, "an expert" on my little goddess, was that she was about a year and half older than I was. And it was obvious that she wouldn't make a pleasant traveling companion.

To be honest, I didn't like the way she examined the back compartment, which I'd converted into a bed, and the middle seat, which would serve as her bed, as she looked around the interior of Icarus. Nor could I stomach the cold way she looked at the box of diving equipment and the minibar, one of the things I'd taken the greatest care to set up. Although I showed

her around Icarus in a gruff manner myself, determined that I
wouldn't travel with someone who didn't want to travel with me,
I was already making a list in my mind of the things I would
have to put up with on a trip like this.

My job, which required frequent field studies and business
trips, and my hobby as a scuba diver, had trained me to adapt to
nearly any environment. As always, the biggest obstacle was not
physical conditions but rather people. I wasn't fussy, even when
traveling with someone so pathological that he had to wash a
towel after each use and hang it so that no corners stuck out, and
a colleague who saw his companion as a personal secretary and
expected me to wait on him just because he was good-looking
and popular with women. But I had resolved in my mind that I
wouldn't let someone who had no interest in diving, no curiosity
about the world underwater, ride in Icarus. From the one or two
things she'd let slip, while reminiscing about the past, I gathered
that her life, on the whole, had nothing to do with the sea,
except for the nickname, Conch, which my little goddess had
given her because of the shape of her ears. When I mentioned
diving, she took it to mean that I liked fishing, and said sarcasti-
cally that mackerel, pikes, and anchovies were about the only fish
she could identify. But that was okay. I would amend my rules.

Something that did require a specific solution was my sleeping habit of going to bed naked. I couldn't fall asleep otherwise. On this trip with Conch in Icarus, I would probably have
to change this practice, painful as that would be. When I first
started dating Pink Anemone, we stayed in the same room once
on a business trip, and I opted to stay up all night. As exhausted
as I was from the day's labor, I chose to talk through the night
with her rather than toss and turn, clothed in bed. Thanks to
that, my relationship with Pink Anemone made rapid progress,
but there was no telling whether my sleeping habit would benefit

me in such a way while traveling with this woman, Conch. I pictured myself, having parked Icarus at the foot of a mountain at night, staring at the thick, dark shadow of a tree in my sleepless anxiety.

To overcome my uncertainties, I told myself the following: "While traveling, I'll suggest, in stages, that Conch take up scuba diving, and I'll be willing to teach her if she does decide to take it up. I'll patiently explain to this woman who knows nothing of the sea about the surface and the inside of the sea, about the organisms that live underwater, about the furies of the sea. I'll learn to be patient enough to deal with her cynicism and arrogance. I won't neglect to make preparations, little by little, and when I'm ready, probably, I'll be able to see my little goddess again. I'll change my sleeping habits as well. I'll let Conch have the thick goose down sleeping bag, which I bought when I bought Icarus, and I'll sleep in layers of thick clothing without a blanket. There might be three or four days when I'll have to go off to an inn by myself. Everything will be difficult at first. But I'll think of the little goddess who had made her way to me in a path of blue water, cutting through a patch of clear sunlight. If only I could see my little goddess again by doing so. And if only, some day, I could descend peacefully with her into the splendid blue underwater world, just once."

Thus, I made up my mind to take a trip with Conch in Icarus, not knowing how long it would be.

Conch

I NEVER LOOK back. And I have no regrets. Even if misjudg-
ment on my part has made some things go wrong. Everything is
determined by desire. On reflection, my desires have always been
simple, and now they've become even simpler. For a desire to
become burning energy, it's first purified, in a simple, primitive
way, and once it starts to burn, it burns down all the rules of
daily life. I, Conch, had to go in search of Jini now, as everyone
else had given up on it, and nothing else made me feel so alive.

At the first rest stop on the southbound lane of the Gyeongbu
Expressway, I waited for him, as if testing myself for having
decided to go on a trip with a man of uncertain identity, trusting
him based on nothing more than the look in his eyes. I wouldn't
wait a single extra minute. If something came up that would
make him late for something like this, then it was meant to be.
I tried to appease myself, telling myself that, growing more and
more anxious as the appointed hour approached. The air, which
oppressed my body with a bleak chill that seemed to foretell early
snow, made me strangely nostalgic for a bygone time, touching
upon lost memories of early winter days a year or two before. I
recalled trivial things: the movement of Jini's hair as she turned
her head; the traces of a faint smile; the unique curves of her
calves; the movement of her hand, which she placed on her eyes

when she fell asleep. This was not the kind of mood I preferred to be in.

But I hadn't been wrong, as I found out. At nine a.m. sharp, the hour I'd appointed, I saw the man's car enter the rest stop. I couldn't help but recognize it. It looked even more ridiculous from far away. Never once had I thought that I would meet someone who drove such a gaudy, flamboyant car, much less go on a trip with him. But I'd made up my mind not to obsess over the nonessential. I had no interest in what kind of person he was, what kind of past he had. What mattered to me on this trip was that we had the same interest, and that we had something to do together. If ever that changed, I would put an end to the trip without a second thought.

I thought of this man as an SOS signal from Jini. If you ask me for proof, I have nothing to offer. No one in this world has the right to demand proof of the communion between Jini and me. The man had no mark whatsoever of someone with an extraordinary mission. Nothing but wrinkles on his brows, like a banana leaf, often found in those who are sensitive and fastidious. He looked no different from the first day I met him—an ordinary man you'd just pass by, whether from up close or far away. But something behind his appearance moved me to action. I'm not sure what that is yet. If I had any interest in him at all, it was because I wanted to understand why, of all people, Jini had chosen and sent him to me. For that reason, I'd spent nearly half a day with a man I'd never met before.

I decided to call him by his diving nickname, Lionfish. It was a bit complicated, but I didn't want to make a fuss over something like that. I didn't care about his real name, his education, his past, his background. So I decided to forget his real name. Frankly speaking, with Lionfish, I enjoyed talking about Jini for the first time in my life. And I realized something I myself had been unaware of. I realized for the first time that I had almost never spoken openly about Jini, other than for business related reasons, to emphasize her value as a model, to give advice on advertisements for ways to bring out the best in her, or to land the perfect job for her; and that talking to someone about the Jini that only I knew and could describe—how she looked when she was happy or sad, the pink of her flushed cheeks when she was in an awkward situation, the sweet tickle when she wrote on my palm, the strange light that spread out through her entire body when she was being mischievous—brought me great pleasure. What could be more absurd than this? I'd never enjoyed such simple pleasure with anyone, not Agar-Agar, or Starfish, or Shark. Why was that? What had gone wrong, and how?

But the man, Lionfish, whose movements were remarkably well-trained despite his appearance, listened to my words about Jini like a thirsty, dying man gulping down water, like someone receiving a crucial command. It was no good talking to him about Jini, dancing an exotic dance, holding a cup of imported coffee, whose brand was designed for popular appeal; Jini with a charming smile on her face, texting a man while sitting at the prow of a boat at night; Jini holding in her hands bottles of lotion that would make all the men in the world stand upright; Jini, fossilized on the screen, everything about her calculated for an effect—the subtlety of the expression on her face, the angles of her arms, and finer details. That wasn't the Jini that drew his attention. He didn't hide his disappointment when I talked about Jini in that way, and acted as if he didn't know what I was talking about. He was hungry to learn about other aspects of Jini.

I should probably say that I discovered the pleasure of talking about Jini while trying, in a subtle way, to find out what it was that Lionfish wanted to learn. I couldn't help but feel convinced, once again, that he was a messenger sent by Jini. I went on talking endlessly about all the different aspects of Jini, which, though trivial, were vividly imprinted in my memory and sustained me daily after she left, and for that very reason made me despair when I longed for her intensely. The reason why I suggested that we go in search of Jini together probably had more to do with this pleasure I'd just discovered, which seemed more meaningful to me than any other criterion of judgment, than the effect his remodeled car had on me.

I picked up the small bag I had put on the ground, and walked up to Lionfish, who had just gotten out of the car and was scanning the rest stop. When he saw me, he expressed his pleasure through an overwhelmed expression and gesture, as if something incredible he had only dreamed of had actually come to pass. Without much ado, I looked at the face of this man who was smiling awkwardly at me. I looked straight into his eyes. I stared at him until I could see a mysterious orange object in his pupils. And I could tell that this man wasn't lying, that he wasn't using Jini as an excuse to procrastinate and put off his life, forgiving his own monstrosity with infinite mercy, as some people do. I could also tell that this somewhat shy man, who seemed to be a good person, with good manners, was by no means someone to think lightly of; that he had a poisonous thorn hidden within himself, somewhere deep down and invisible. I also knew, however, that the poison could turn out to be something insignificant once he found what he was looking for. Thus I perceived that the poisonous thorn pricking at him inside had arisen from a sense of the emptiness of life, a fundamental sense of loss. I couldn't just pass by someone like that, not I. I climbed into the conspicuous, strange-looking car, which he insisted that I call Icarus, whose door he'd left open.

I sat in the passenger seat, of course. The seat would be mine for a while now. Until we met Jini again, or until our common purpose lost its meaning, through whoever's fault, and we no longer had a reason for traveling together. I took another look inside Icarus, as if visiting my new home. I would try, little by little, to get used to the interior, which was simply furbished. Unlike the exterior, this interior that made me picture two or three close friends having a quiet drink or tea together, with the car parked in a shadow at the foot of a mountain after a long trip, or a couple lying down, listening to music, then making love, rather than a fussy trip with family or colleagues. Icarus, which reminded me more of suspension than movement, and night more than day, began to speed up quietly.

I didn't say anything. Lionfish kept silent as well. The silence wasn't one of anxiety and uneasiness that falls between strangers, but a peaceful one, tainted by nothing. Lionfish and I each withdrew into ourselves. Icarus moved forward noiselessly, which you wouldn't expect by looking at its exterior or size; inside the car, only the sound of jazz music Lionfish had turned on slipped into my thoughts now and then. I closed my eyes and focused my mind, as if doing that would let me see Jini, walking somewhere. The music faded gradually, and I meandered into a vacuous scene, although I don't know if you could call a space in which there was no person, color, or object a scene. I stayed for a while in that colorless, formless space. Perhaps I fell asleep.

When I opened my eyes again, I pulled out from my bag the map I'd brought, feeling as if I could find somewhere like the scene I'd experienced with my eyes closed. With the intuition of a hunting dog, I looked at the roads on the map, waiting for a meaningful sign to reveal itself. No memory of Jini, no matter how specific, could help me much at times like this, as the memories were wordless, like scenes from silent films. Jini had never said anything about a trip. It was always just me wanting to go on a trip, wandering around, just the two of us, in search of a world where she could find her true self.

I found on the map roads along railroad tracks. Roads around the tracks in directions of the west and east coasts, particularly ones nearest to the shores. I knew, though Jini had never said anything, that if she was headed somewhere, she'd be moving from one train station to another, and from the train, she'd be able to see the ocean in the distance through the window. I saw an exit sign ahead on the highway. I said to Lionfish, "Make an exit there and take a route close to the beach. I don't have to take the freeway to get anywhere. Do you?"

Instead of answering, Lionfish changed lanes without a moment's delay and got ready to exit the highway. Secretly admiring the fluidity of Icarus as it wheeled toward the west coast, I felt an encouraging sense of excitement fill me little by little, and that this trip with Lionfish would proceed smoothly.

She Saw the Moonlight Shattering
on the Square Fountain

WHAT MADE PEOPLE start dancing? Was there joy in the beginning? A fear of the universe? Respect for life? Or was it sorrow for extinction that made them dance?

What made her start dancing? Was there, inside her body, something that couldn't be put into words making her dance? Did some kind of ecstasy only she could feel turn her movements, so simple, into a dance? People who saw her dance for the first time could not help but ask these questions. The happiness of her dance, and the unhappiness, lay in its ability to go back to the beginning and call forth what had become eroded by time and hidden behind chaotic events. Thus were there people who, after having seen her dance once, could never forget it. On nights when they, for some reason, had trouble falling asleep, they pictured her dancing, and with a peaceful smile headed straight to the realm of sleep. At times, those who foolishly wanted proof followed after her, thinking she'd dance again sometime. But she only very rarely danced. So they each returned to their life, to offices, markets, streets. Not everyone, however, felt the same way. Among those who'd seen her dance, some left in a frantic rush, feeling uncomfortable and out of sorts. But those who came back to see her dance again, could never leave her again.

No one took statistics, but those who saw her dance were so rare that they could be counted on ten fingers. The woman she met on the beach was probably the fifth or sixth. She spent some time, not too long, at the bleak, empty house with the dog and the unhappy couple, for how many days she didn't know but until the woman no longer imagined that she was her daughter.

No room or house seemed unfamiliar to her anymore. In the room of the woman's daughter, where she stayed, there were photographs of the previous occupant of the room, who had melancholy features, and looked a year or two older than she was, and some luxurious belongings of a girl around her age, who had left her parents early on. They didn't really bother her. The woman's daughter, dating a well-known local playboy, swept all the family jewelry into her boyfriend's bag and disappeared without a trace one night on the motorboat her boyfriend had stolen. Every day, when the day began to turn into evening, the woman began to keep a watch on the room, which troubled her, and didn't stop until deep into the night, for at the hour when her daughter had gone out, supposedly to see a friend in the neighborhood, her daughter would run off somewhere.

The woman's days, however, started very late, as she had insomnia and went to bed late. During the day, she once again became the ordinary wife of a community leader, as quiet and unassuming as her elegant hair. Occasionally, one or two women, along with an old woman, came to visit, to learn calligraphy. And on some days, the woman would go on touching up her hair, which she had already taken hours to put up in a knot, then fall into a long nap. The woman's days were so tranquil that it seemed as if all the misfortune in the world stay away from her.

She didn't know what it was that kept her at this house. It was probably the dog that lingered around her. The backyard of the house, full of all kinds of trees, and built by the woman's reticent, ever-rueful husband, who'd been born in the region and found success in the transportation business, brought her comfort; walking all afternoon among the trees in the spacious backyard with the dog was the only pleasure she enjoyed while staying at the house.

The dog was the only audience watching her dance when the wind passed through the yard, where there was no one else. The breeze in the air, the water of the sea, and images that appeared and disappeared in her mind—these were the materials for her dance. Sometimes, she saw a shadow hovering on the glass door of the woman's room, which opened to the backyard. But her dance did not interfere with the woman's sleep or quiet activities during the day, and although she herself was not aware, it might have been for the woman that she danced.

The woman's delusion was as deep as her sorrow for losing her daughter, but fortunately, it didn't last long. Peace, however, did not come at no cost. One late afternoon, when the dusk fell thicker than usual and the old pine trees in the yard seemed ablaze, the woman beat the dog and dragged her by her thick, long hair, going around and around the yard of the big house. Her body was rumpled and dashed to the ground, and picked up only to be dumped again, like a rag doll being abused at the hands of a finicky child who no longer had love in her heart. The dog and she both endured quietly through the woman's painful outburst, which lasted for how long, they didn't know, and would be recalled hundreds of times later, as is each single act of undeserved violence.

What the woman found afterward was a wretched peace. The woman nursed the wounds she herself had inflicted, but no one knew if they would heal without scars. The woman did not wail and lament, or shed tears of regret, but a strange indifference, found occasionally in those who have committed something that would make it impossible for them to be their old selves again, showed her pain more clearly than ever. The woman caressed her body, kissed her wounds, and shed a single drop of tear; then she collapsed into sleep next to her. As the woman slept with her mouth open, looking too overwhelmed to face the world, which had reassembled itself the moment she finally accepted that she had lost something after denying it for so long, she got to her feet.

Her bones seemed to rattle, and her flesh screamed in pain, but she realized that for the peace of the woman beside her to last, she had to stand up, now. The dog, limping, walked on ahead of her. The moonlight, thicker and milkier than usual, turned the woods an even darker green this night. With the dog showing the way, she walked the long path she'd always traveled by car with the woman. Whenever she took a step forward, a red light went on in all the joints in her body, signaling danger and making the sharp pain transparent.

When they had walked for a while, a car stopped next to them. She and the dog got in the car, belonging to the woman's husband who was on his way home. Shocked, he wanted to take her to a nearby hospital, but she firmly refused and asked him silently to keep driving. Whenever they came to a fork, she raised a hand to indicate the direction. They drove on for several hours in this way. Whenever a wave of sleep came over her, making her want to let herself go, the dog did all it could to breathe some strength into her, sniffing at her cheek.

When a little city came into view, she pressed her face against the window and looked outside, as if searching for something. Then the city would disappear, and another city would appear.

After they'd passed many such cities with little clusters of light, she gently placed her hand on the driver's shoulder, and pointed to a little square outside the window with her finger. The car stopped, and she got out. The dog, as always, just stared at her, and the man, about to say something, swallowed his words and waved goodbye. The car slowly circled around the square, and got back on the path it had traveled.

She liked the little square of the sleepy town. Here, she felt she could stay until the wounds on her body healed. She would be left with scars, of course. Especially from the wound around her eyebrow, where the blood had just stopped, and which the inflictor herself had nursed. But there was no telling if the wound would leave a lazy curve that would make her beautiful eyes even warmer, more mellow. And she had finally become void. She no longer had anything to carry in her hands or on her back, to keep or throw away.

Listening to the sound the water made, shooting up, then falling on the surface, she looked around the fountain, then into the distance. She hadn't been mistaken. The beds of flowers under the streetlamps, the trees planted along the path around the fountain, which shed leaves whenever the wind blew, the mountains in the distance which stood with their backs to the square, and the smell in the air told her that the city was very close to the sea. A child's bicycle stood in a corner of the empty square, forgotten rather than abandoned. The metal wheels shone in the moonlight, and the moonlight shattered brilliantly against the water that spurted from the little fountain, probably designed to celebrate an important event.

Starfish

REALLY, I WANTED to live a quiet life. If I had a life plan, it was to look after my lonely self while young, find a quiet house on the outskirts of a city, where nameless wildflowers grew tangled together, and live and die without anyone knowing. I had no greed, ambitions, or aspirations. I learned early on that things like that are dangerous. Being with a man now and then would be all right, if he could satisfy my simple needs for food, clothing, and shelter, and provide me with a few luxuries, no different from what everyone wants. And for him to be generous enough to humor me when, every once in a while, I get difficult, it wouldn't hurt for him to be rich. Rich enough to let me enjoy, without working, the ordinary comforts the world provides. Yes, that would be nice. I wanted to grow old gracefully like that. Making it my goal to not turn into a nasty old woman.

That was about all there was to the dreams and wishes I could imagine for myself, but everything started to change.

I had made up my mind to live a quiet life, gulping down whatever horrible truth there was in the world. I know that no one wants to face the truth. My short life experience has taught me that it takes a lot of work to face the truth, and it doesn't really pay. I don't mean to say, though, that I'm hiding something that has to be exposed. I'm just saying, fair is fair. I could

probably be happy without men, without you, people like you
who bring me simple daily pleasures now and then. Growing
old gracefully by myself. But that one phone call began to ruin
my tranquility.

The call came right after Shark went out. It was from an
advertiser who'd given Jini one or two jobs. I'd met him, too, of
course. He was good-looking, had a ponytail, and was wearing a
thick, clunky silver ring on his chubby index finger, which wasn't
a pretty sight. He once lunged at Shark, shaking in the air the
contract that had turned useless with Jini's disappearance. Shark
sat there for nearly two hours, not even batting an eye. Afraid
something like that might happen again, I told him Shark was
out, but it was me he wanted to see. If I have one weakness, it's
that I have a hard time refusing anyone who wants me. So I
accepted his proposal that we meet.

In a sweet voice, he suggested that I take Jini's place. This
when I wanted to live a quiet life, scoffing at the people of the
world who clung so desperately to little things. He was persua-
sive, and promised that if everything went well, he would "fetch"
me other jobs as well. I don't know why, but I listened to his
words with a sad look on my face, the look of someone who was
grieving her sister's death. He talked a lot. You know the kind of
people who believe that things turn out better the more you talk.
He said that people were waiting. He raved about how the results
would be beyond expectations if I stepped forward when everyone wanted to see Jini again. On top of that, he added, what I
had to do was quite simple. According to him, I just had to sit on
a rock and strike a couple of poses. They would use some of Jini's
videos in part, for special effect, but I needn't worry, because
they had methods to take care of it. The ad was for shoes. What
mattered here were the knees and the calves. He said he'd gotten
a good look at those parts of my body the last time he came to

visit. I suppose I could say that it was a good thing that my first job required parts of my body that were pretty decent.

At first, I was nervous. Taking Jini's place was a world of difference from following her around, running little errands. After five-and-a-half hours of posing for just thirty seconds of footage, the ponytail finally gave an okay signal, and feeling satisfied, he took me home. He wanted to keep working with me, he was saying. He really liked me. That's how I happened to plunge into this crazy world. Well, I guess I couldn't say that it was completely unexpected. And I couldn't say that I hadn't made any preparations. Anyway, I really did want to live in quiet, and still do . . . . But as ponytail said, what can I do, when people want me?

After my first job, things became clear to me, little by little. I told Shark only after I had done the deed. I thought he'd get angry, but he just looked piercingly into my eyes and didn't say a word. Then he called ponytail and made an appointment in that impatient voice of his. It was probably to make sure that nothing was amiss with Jini's video copyrights and my contract. That's how it began. It was very easy. Shark went to talk to Conch about the next step. But Conch's room was empty. She never had that much stuff to begin with, but until that moment, we hadn't realized that her room was completely empty, that she'd gone off somewhere without telling us. Shark looked me up and down with sharp eyes, as if he were seeing me for the first time. My back broke out in a cold sweat, as if I had bullets flying at me. Finally, Shark withdrew his gaze and shrugged, then looked at me with a bit of contempt. It was the look he got on his face from time to time when faced with something of poor quality.

"You are Starfish, after all!" he said.

Then his face took on a gloomy, defeated look. He spat out, "You should start out with something sappy."

I hate my family sometimes. I can see right through them. The gloom on Shark's face, I know what it's saying: It's no use trying, Starfish. But just wait and see. I'm going to stomp all over that face sometime. I'm going to do everything in my power to make that look of gloom into a look of even greater contempt, into the most terrific look of disappointment. When that time comes, no one will associate me with Jini.

Several days later at the instruction of Shark, I successfully filmed a television show that would let the people craving after Jini lose themselves in the grief of a girl who'd lost her little sister forever. Jini's videos took up more than half the film, of course. I mourned Jini's death with my body and soul, as if burying her for good, as I had done while sitting in a dark room, watching her videos. Do you know how much more energy it takes to act out grief than joy? As soon as I came home, I collapsed and slept for more than two days. When I woke up, I was sick for a long time and threw everything up. That was the last of it. I'm not going to throw up what I swallow ever again.

I have no illusions. Starting out was easy, but for a while, things are going to be just that hard. It isn't easy being in Jini's shadow even after she's gone. But the day will come when I'm going to swallow the shadow, all of it. Soon the shadow will be forgotten. And I can gulp everything down because my tears will let people know that Jini has died somewhere. It'll be only as unpleasant as swallowing something bitter. Days will pass, one by one, without incident if I curb my temper, bite my tongue, and live against my nature.

But why do you have to swallow well to live well? Why do you have to overcome?

She Found Her Lost Voice

THE FOUNTAIN AT noon was simple and transparent. No matter what shadowy transactions and affairs may be taking place in the back alleys of the city, the fountain in the square greeted her with a quiet, subtle sound of breathing that could be heard only at that hour, as if it had been waiting for her by itself. The winter was deepening, but it wasn't cold in the city. The fountain water, which shot up in little, slow spurts, then flew in a downward arc, neither froze nor dried up. She sat on the edge of the fountain, bathing in the sun and observing the changes in the shape, color, and line of the water as it spurted out, which fascinated her all the more because they were so fine, and waited for some emotion, like sorrow at times, and longing at times, to fill up inside her, drop by drop.

No one knew where she lived. But every day at noon she appeared at the square without fail. No one noticed her coming, but she would suddenly be a part of the scene around the fountain, as if someone had transported her out of nowhere. The fountain was an important signpost for her in her day. But for some reason, no one dared go near her. Enchanted by the sight of her, people would stop and gaze as she basked in the sun, but didn't approach her or talk to her. It wasn't that they knew she had lost her voice. Those who had stopped before her once or

twice were waiting for something. They waited in silence. For her
to rise, for her beautiful body to move. For her to show them the
marvelous movements of her body they once saw, which drew
them toward the fountain.

When she felt that she'd gotten enough sun, she quietly rose
and began to dance. Her dance began with a sort of flutter, like
that of wings, slow and unstable. Then it took on the speed and
motion of a repetitive routine. She danced this dance dozens of
times, hundreds of times on some days. But it changed slightly
each time. Her dance conveyed a different message and feeling
every time, and people didn't realize that her movements were,
in the end, the same.

As her dance reached its peak, the crowd that had gathered
around the fountain would begin to form a little circle around
her, making it seem as if the city were waking up from a nap. As
she danced, her lips seemed to say something, or sing the words
of a song with a regular rhythm. In the shape of her lips, through
which no sound emerged, people found the words they wanted
to hear. Old people, who had a lot of time and came to see her
dance every day, could not skip even a single day because it
seemed to them that she whispered the words they most wanted
to hear again: "Don't be afraid, You'll pass into the next world
in peace, as if in your sleep, as if flying."

Her words rang in the ears in a voice most pleasant to the
listener, in a tone so soft and gentle that it seemed to caress the
flesh. Those who received the wordless message would make
an exclamation that sounded like a groan or a sigh. Thus they
gave back to her the voice she had lost. Market vendors, passing
through from time to time, stopped before her as well.

"You have nothing to worry about at the next market. Bear
with it just a little longer," they seemed to hear. They would
hasten their steps toward their shops, hands in pockets, lest

their sudden good mood be spoiled. Young women around her age stood huddled in groups, sipping coffee or tea in paper cups, hiding their admiration as they watched her supple, flawless body.

"You don't see yourself, so far away that no worry can reach you."

"Forget about it. Everything will be all right."

Her lip messages and the language of her dance changed every day, but the same feeling emanated from the faces and steps of those who left the area around the fountain. A feeling that the messages they had received as they watched her dance weren't so different from one another. It was a joy at times, a light excitement at times, a peaceful smile or look of deep thought at times that showed on people's faces. An incident that occurred one day served to spread the knowledge of her dance, as sorrow and pain always express themselves in exaggerated ways, whereas happiness makes its way among people without color and shape, leaving only a slight trace.

The day was sunny, and the sky dry and blue, as if determined to present the wintriest scene possible; people couldn't attribute what they experienced that day to bad weather. As always, she began to dance slowly, her eyes closed and lips touched by a faint smile, as if she didn't see those who had gathered around the fountain. The smile, the kind that might rest on your lips after you've endured through a painful, difficult time, went well with her dance that day. The smile became a part of her dance and captivated the audience. And then it happened. The small and simple audience that had been watching her dance began to weep simultaneously. The quiet sorrow grew more and more intense. Some began to sob so loudly that she had to come to a stop. But the tears weren't necessarily tears of sorrow. As the people left the area, they looked refreshed, as if old impurities had been purged from their bodies. Regardless of what may be said of the tears, they overpowered the people for a long while and served to bring more people to the fountain area the next day, and the day after that.

The fountain area, where people stopped for a while before going off again, after which other people arrived, was strangely tranquil. When she began to dance, people felt as if all noise stopped in the square, and an exceptional vacuous atmosphere was created. It became a custom for them to leave coins or bills before they left, on the slab of marble surrounding the fountain, something that took place in that square only around that hour. When the crowd had left one by one and only a few people remained, scattered here and there, one of them would gather the coins and bills and place them in one spot. People watched her, forgetting the cold, the time, even themselves. Things hadn't always proceeded in this way, of course. Some people in the beginning had even picked up the coins on the ground and disappeared. But the next day, and the day after that, they would come back and quietly return what they'd taken, something else you could see only there.

After she finished dancing, she would sit on the edge of the fountain, her head lowered for a moment as she caught her breath. In that moment, her eyes looked moist, as if shrouded in a mist, and sometimes she would smile in a way that would make anyone who had seen the smile once come back to the place. Sometimes, though very rarely, her upper body would shake as she leaned against the cold rock surrounding the fountain and wept fiercely without sound. But no one, kind as they were, dared approach her to comfort her or ask what was wrong. They left one by one, leaving her alone. They knew that there was nothing they could do for her. She left without being noticed, just as she did when she came to the fountain, and became a part of the busy, crowded street, and disappeared somewhere without a trace.

Conch

OH, THE BEAUTY of an empty road on a winter night! Even if this trip came to an end without us achieving our purpose, I'll take away with me, etched in my body, some beautiful scenes that cannot be removed from my memory. Especially some scenes of night and dawn. But these few comforts don't mean that this trip has been a smooth ride. I didn't think I'd have a problem getting used to any fussy habits of my traveling companion, but that turned out to be a hasty conclusion. Lionfish was a tricky man, like a lawn hiding landmines. But I'm no fool. There's no need to touch a spot where I know a landmine is buried. He couldn't stand it when I asked him anything about his private life before he met Jini. As time went on, he opened up completely about Jini, telling me that he called her little goddess, even that he closed his eyes and pictured her in his mind before falling asleep. On the other hand, I was to show no interest whatsoever in his past. His attitude seemed to say, "I don't want to share anything with you, Conch, besides stories about my little goddess." That was fine. I didn't care about anything other than Jini, either. But the past and the present aren't divided into two distinct parts like that, are they? The two were bound to merge as we talked, and Lionfish loathed this merging, as if it were a bad omen.

The uncomfortable feeling that fell between us, about three days after we had set out, was intensified by the irritation he showed when physically exhausted. Although he had no intention of having someone else take over the driving, he couldn't stand the fact that he was stuck with someone who didn't do anything and became testy. He was defying me because I told him to change directions and to drive deep into the night, or all night, as my fancy dictated, without regard to his condition, even though I myself didn't even know how to drive. But no matter. I still had the initiative on this trip. I knew how to appease the anxiety eating away at his mind when he was feeling tense and worn out. When I told him stories about Jini, he grew meek and tender so immediately that it was astonishing. I don't know how many nights and how long a distance he drove Icarus while drunk on my stories about Jini.

To be honest, I liked how well he drove at night. He was very gentle, yet decisive. I would bury myself deep in the comfortable seat of Icarus, forgetting the unsettling possibilities regarding Jini's situation, as well as my worries about my uncertain future, and would start talking about Jini.

"If I ever become famous, Lionfish, it'll be because of my book on Jini, which I'm determined to write one day . . . One late afternoon long ago, when the world began to tilt all of a sudden, I met Jini for the first time in a dark valley. I was trying to decide whether to give up my life or continue living when I sensed someone watching me and turned my head. There I saw the beautiful, sympathetic smile of a little girl. And in that moment, my life changed . . ."

That was the kind of opening and tone Lionfish liked, very solemn. It wasn't what I preferred, but I didn't mind humoring him now and then. Telling him about Jini in different ways, I myself was looking for the tone most suitable in describing her, the sequence of my memories of her, and the emotional moments that couldn't and shouldn't be forgotten. Whenever we faced a difficulty on the trip, I thought to myself that the trip was a step toward writing my book on Jini. The hope that all these memories occupying my mind would come to life someday gave me the patience necessary to endure the conflicts with Lionfish.

The trip hasn't been smooth, by any means, and won't be in the future. There were moments when Lionfish was so cruel that I clenched my teeth, vowing that I would put an end to the trip immediately. Not knowing what it was in me that triggered this attitude of his, I waited for the moment to pass. I didn't have much savings or cash, as I'd thought I would be with Jini for the rest of my life. Lionfish and I had a tacit agreement to share traveling expenses until we found Jini, but on the second day of the trip, I realized that I'd been greatly mistaken. Icarus required at least three times my usual expenses to run properly, and Lionfish's standard of living wasn't easy for someone like me to live up to. Knowing this, Lionfish offered no help moneywise when his mood turned nasty for whatever reason. Sometimes, I watched him eat, just sipping water myself, or waited out in the street while he was in a pub drinking, wondering how much he squandered on drinks in just one evening.

What was the most difficult to bear were the dead hours when no insight or knowledge came to me. During our stay in an area, we go around, at my instruction, where people gather and inquire about any tidbit of information on Jini, or any young woman who could be Jini.

I packed a number of Jini's photographs in my bag, of course, before setting out, but I had never imagined thrusting those photographs at strangers. How should I explain it? Like people in the past who thought of photographs and paintings as sprits, I was reluctant to expose Jini to everyone in that way, afraid the exposure would wear away at her soul. When I learned that Jini, who I always saw on screens, was gone from me, it even felt like a fact. I felt as if she'd just worn out and disappeared. Neither Lionfish nor I, of course, did anything so foolish as to go to the police station in the town or city where we were staying and have an official notice issued.

I, at least, insisted on finding Jini through my means alone. For me, the process of finding her was like that of solving a riddle. Some people, though very few, said they'd seen someone who could be Jini. But I didn't really trust the information they provided. This attitude of mine was something that often jarred against Lionfish. He pressed me with questions at times, suspicious that I was deliberately keeping us from finding Jini. I suspected at times that he saw me as some kind of parasite, enjoying a leisurely road trip and whiling away time, using Jini as an excuse. But there was no way that a misunderstanding like that could hurt me; I'd been misunderstood too many times for that. I trusted only one thing: the reaction of my body when sensing that I was nearer to, or farther from, Jini. I suppose you could say that I was arrogant, expecting I would run miraculously into Jini on the street one day, relying on my feelings and intuition alone.

Such a miracle hasn't occurred yet. Not yet.

She Danced an Unstoppable Dance

IT WASN'T NECESSARILY around the fountain that the biggest crowd gathered. And she wasn't necessarily looking for a place with a big crowd. If a market was held in the small town to the south, she went there. Like a plant that seeks light, she went in search of people gathered at the market. Her dance began in a corner of the market, noticed by no one, then people began to gather one by one to watch. She always danced barefoot, with her eyes closed. The sight of her dancing barefoot in winter on the stone pavement around the fountain made those watching recall the most uncomfortable, shameful thoughts hidden in the recesses of their minds, of which everyone had at least one. But they didn't resent her.

The expression on her face remained the same, except on very rare occasions. She danced with an absorbed look on her face that couldn't be described as one of either peace or joy. Those who had seen her dance always stopped before her again, at least once. Not everyone, though, stopped to watch her every time, or for long. So the circle of people around her, whether it was around the fountain, or in the market streets, was always small.

There was a girl who always appeared in the circle of people that formed wherever she danced. The young girl, small in stature, whose exact age could not be discerned, squeezed her way in through the people to see the young woman dance, looking thin and expressionless. She always had a small water bottle at her side, which she held in her hand as if aiming at something, as if it were a gun or a knife. People felt threatened by her posture, and looked at the water bottle before they looked at her face.

The vacant look on her face, which didn't suit a young girl, was so peculiar that it drew people in. The girl, who still had flushed baby cheeks, always had something bulging from her back. Both her face and body looked so young that people wondered if what she was carrying under the baby blanket, big enough to cover the girl, was a live baby or a doll the size of a baby, with a loosely-knit woolen hat pulled over its head. People hastily made room for the small young girl, with a face so devoid of expression that it scared them, who might have come to watch the dance with a baby sibling on her back. Then the girl slipped out of the crowd and stood alone at a distance, her feet apart as if to bear the weight of the load on her back, watching the dance without budging. She looked like a warrior, her weapon loaded, ready to attack an invisible enemy. Sometimes, the dancer looked at no one but the girl as she danced, but even then, no change came over the girl's expression.

What the girl was carrying on her back was a real, breathing baby, who squirmed at times, and whimpered at times. The girl seemed accustomed to the baby, as to a lump on her back, didn't hoist the blanket back up even when it slid down below her slender waist, and paid no attention to the baby's reaction to anything, if she could help it. But when the baby began to howl, she deftly brought it to her chest with a movement that looked odd somehow, and unbuttoned her shirt and suckled it. Her swollen breasts, which looked as if they had been grafted to her lean upper body, hung from her as awkwardly and precariously as the baby sucking at her emaciated body. When the girl thrust her breasts, exceptionally large for a girl her age, at the baby, it stopped howling. The breasts were the saddest sight in the world the dancer had ever glimpsed.

At first, she stopped dancing for a moment, standing before the girl who was unbuttoning her shirt, paying no attention to the people watching. But a look in the eyes of the girl who lifted her head again and watched her, with the baby sucking her breasts, which hadn't been there before, made her go on dancing. The eyes seemed to say, "Please keep dancing. This is the only time in the day when I feel any hope at all."

The people who had whispered in the beginning grew accustomed to the girl as she kept returning, and in their whispering, her past was created. There's no knowing whether the girl, who stayed even after everyone had scattered away, and squeezed her way in only after people had gathered, knew about the rumors that grew in whispers. But it wasn't always through words that things were conveyed to her.

The girl, who looked ordinary, with a disproportionate body often found in kids around her age, and dressed in the shabbiest of clothes, grew up in a city not too far from the town, a big city where the greatest misfortune in the world had at one time taken place. But she could no longer live in that city, where her old mother, who had taken the girl into her care after she was born, had lived. The girl's mother, who was already quite aged when the girl first met her, an old woman, almost, lost her struggle against sorrow in the end and died.

The girl had heard only a part of the sad story from her mother. Her mother told her that long before the girl was born, her father and older brother, whom she'd never even met, had been taken from the city without a trace as were countless people, and not even a funeral could be held for them. Her mother, who had once taught children, began to tell the girl when she was just barely beginning to understand words: "Even just a few years before you were born, we were living in a primitive age. The spirit of the age was so strong that those who tried to free themselves of it and live like decent human beings were all killed. People begin to gradually awaken in the face of death, which is both their limit and misfortune. You have work to do when you grow up. You must find a way for people to become wise, without going through death and destruction."

The girl, however, grew slowly, and the joy she brought her mother must have been inadequate for dispelling sorrow, for her mother passed away when the girl was just beginning to understand what the words meant. Her mother's sorrow must have been profound judging from the way she wept even how she drew her last breath. Having to survive day by day, the girl couldn't even think about her mother's wishes, and when she tried to recall those wishes, she got a splitting headache and had to think about something else. Her mother left her very little, and she barely managed to finish elementary school. Her mother's sorrow gradually infected her, and the city became unbearable for her, as she had memories of her mother, as well as memories of her mother's memories.

The girl, alone again, left the city to work in a famous sashimi restaurant in the town, with the help of a relative who had looked after her mother. But the girl became pregnant one day, and when her belly was so swollen that the baby could come out any moment, she was turned out. She could have died in that state, of course, as she lay out in the street for days, not budging and not even covering her swollen, aching belly. Some market people, however, took her in. She was able to give birth to the baby, and helped several households with errands in return for food, and was even allowed to sleep in a warehouse.

No one knew whether these pieces of stories, floating around, were true or not. There were countless pieces of stories, but they were generally patched together in similar ways. They may have been rumors created by someone who had brought her to the restaurants, or someone who had taken her in or abandoned her. Regardless of her past, no one took any interest in her beyond that, and the only thing that was certain was that she was a nuisance in the market streets. It was also true that people couldn't treat her with contempt, because although they didn't know how she had come to live in the city, there was a certain formidable arrogance about her that made the speculations possible, as well as a feeling of privation that came from her current unhappy circumstances. But it could have been the water bottle she carried at her side that they feared the most. Maybe they were afraid of her because of that bottle of water, which some said was poison, and others a drug, and yet others rare spring water, which she held in her hand like a gun or a knife aimed at people.

In any case, the girl roamed the fountain area around the same hour every day, as if she couldn't make it through the day without seeing the dance. On days when the dancer made no appearance around the fountain, people saw the girl lying exhausted on the street. Then when the dancer did appear and began to dance, the girl would rise to her feet as if she'd never been lying on the ground. Her weary gait as she squeezed in among the people with no expression on her face whatsoever, as if she refused any involvement in the world, suddenly took on an unruly spirit fit for a girl her age, and more vigorous than anyone else's. This happened when the dance was over, and people scattered in all directions to return to their daily lives, momentarily set aside, after placing their best offerings on the marble slab surrounding the fountain.

Once or twice, the dancer went on dancing for a long, long time. Her body was exhausted, but she couldn't stop dancing. On those days when she herself didn't know what was happening to her, people left, not waiting as they usually did until she had finished. In the empty square, she danced an unstoppable dance by herself, as she had the first night she was in the city. On such a day, when her entire body was drenched in sweat and her limbs trembled, the girl stayed by her side, watching without moving an inch. Only when she stopped dancing, as if to pass out, and lay down by the fountain, did the girl go up to her, pull out a grubby towel from inside the blanket around her waist, and wipe the cold sweat from her brow.

Shark

I THINK I'VE finally found the island I want to own, the island I must own. The guy boasted excitedly on the other end of the line that the island in question, whose current owner he had found at last, was sure to be the island of my dreams. I don't remember how exactly I described the island I wanted when I asked the guy to find it for me, paying him an exorbitant amount of money. At any rate, when the picture of this island, a little heap of stones in the shape of a rather strange animal, arrived a few days later, my gut told me that I would have to go to this island—which looked rough and desolate as do all islands that haven't been inhabited—and spend the rest of my life there. And that the rest of my life wouldn't be that long.

I don't know how an island like that could have existed till now without being opened to relentless vacationers. Perhaps the fact that it was barren, more like a rock floating around in the sea, and that it belonged to a private owner, were what kept it hidden from people like me. A family who has owned a lot of land in that area for generations bought the island long ago, and the papers had been lying dormant in a drawer belonging to a descendant. I was surprised myself to learn from the guy that there were quite a few people in the world who were off their rockers like me, looking for a desert island. They probably had different reasons, of course, for wanting an island like this. They want an island where water springs and farming is possible, with a great view and rich soil, where trees can grow. If this was the only island that failed to draw people's attention, as the guy said, it went to show just how sterile the environment was. It felt rather lonely not to have any competitors, but I decided to look on the bright side.

I liked the fact that the island was far enough away from land to be invisible on cloudy days. Not only that, it had no name. The guy said that even on the papers, which hadn't been touched since an ancestor, a few generations back, of the current owner had bought it, the island was only marked by its geographical location. Often in such cases, fishermen living in nearby villages would have a nickname for the place, but the guy, somewhat reluctantly, just told me about this rumor: Several men who had gone out to it on a boat had disappeared without a trace. Experienced sailors would go out to the island, but the shape of the island forbade their approach. There were men who brought their boat to a stop near its shores and took a careless step forward; they fell and died as their companions watched. Things like that happened from time to time, and no one who lived nearby had actually been on the island. And when people built a house, they had the door face away from the island, as they saw an ominous animal shape in the island on clear days, when it could be seen in its entirety. They did this because they were superstitious, believing that those who saw the island, regardless of the weather, were always met with catastrophe in the end. That's why no one wanted to name the island. They wanted to turn their backs on it. I could understand. So how could I not like the island?

I asked the guy, who was evasive about the rumors, afraid that I might change my mind, about every little detail. All the problems regarding the island, which he told me with caution, didn't worry me in the least. The more sinister and ominous, the better. As I listened to the rumors he told me about, I felt the bond between myself and the island grow stronger, as if this island in the middle of the ocean had been refusing the approach of others while waiting for me alone. A little piece of barren land full of rocks was making my heart beat intensely for the first time in a while.

If I want, the island will be mine. Never once did something that I wanted, something that I desired, not become mine. Besides, I'm not so stupid as to desire something I can't possess. I know very well how dull and boring are those who waste their lives in anger and anxiety, desiring things they could never have. I decided early on that people like that were to be avoided. And yet I wondered, for many days after the guy called, if it was okay for me to want this island. The price he offered was high enough to make me wonder, and buying an island was only a part of my plan. I'm not going to go live on an isolated island to live a poor, pathetic life. I'll need a state of the art helicopter, a boat that's small but equipped with everything, and I'll need to reshape the island entirely so that I'll be able to live a simple but comfortable life, however many years that might be. Considering all the extra expenses, big and small, I should not want the island.

I gave a general outline of the kind of life I wanted to live on the island to a couple of specialists who aid me whenever I start something, and entrusted them to make a blueprint of a home suitable for such a life, and to round up an estimate of the annual living expenses on the island. I was well aware that my financial situation wouldn't have allowed me to buy the island, let alone live there the way I wanted, for more than two months, at rough estimate, even if the island were to become mine free of charge. But by commissioning the work, I felt that my plans of settling down on a barren island was finally beginning to be realized. It once again made my heart pound, but I was also overcome by a solemn feeling, since I was taking a firm step toward the end of my life.

While my two hardworking friends worked up the estimate, taking my requirements into consideration, I went to see the island, without telling the guy, to cool my head a bit. I was to tell him whether or not to go through with the transaction, as soon as the estimate came through. Luckily, the guy, who went around the country doing stuff like this, had left the village that faced the island and was busy with another transaction. I left my conspicuous sports car behind and took the train, then walked to the seaside village. I rented a room at a fisherman's home and waited for the day to dawn. During my first two days of staying there, the sky was dark and low, as if snow would start falling any minute, and I didn't get to see the sea. But on the third day, I finally did. The weather hadn't cleared up, but I waited, standing on the cold, wet shore, my eyes fixed in the direction of the island. And what I'd been waiting for happened. I saw, in the middle of the sea, the rock island I had seen only pictures of emerge clearly into view from the thick layers of the sea mist. But it was only for a few seconds, at most, that the island revealed itself from the mist, which was dissipated by a momentary puff of sea wind. Once again, the island became shrouded in a thick mist. The few seconds, however, were enough time for me to make up my mind. I had confirmed that the island was just the island I was looking for, the island where I would end my life.

I had no choice but to modify my long-held habit. I didn't ask myself if I was capable enough to want the island. Defying myself, I decided that I wanted the island, and came to this conclusion: I would find a way that would make it okay for me to want this island, and I would be able to live out the rest of my life on the island the way I wanted. But how? I had known from the beginning that there was only one way, from the moment I saw the picture of the island the guy sent me.

She Took a Peek at Herself on the Other Side

AFTER ALL THE people left, there came a moment when her mind went blank, then filled with an indefinable feeling, pinkish-purple in tone. It could be the exhaustion that came over her after dancing with such concentration, or old sorrow stirred up by the exhaustion. In those moments, she couldn't take a single step forward. She would lie down by the fountain and wait, for a certain feeling of solemnity to fill her body, drop by drop. When the weather was warm and mild, the moments grew somewhat shorter. She never appeared in the square when the weather wasn't nice. If it became cloudy while she danced, her moments of rest became prolonged, like the dismal prayers of Agar-Agar that grew little by little in length, almost unnoticed.

When she lifted herself slowly by the fountain, she saw someone hide behind a tree. The day was already drawing to a close. As she got to her feet, she cast a long shadow across the square. She knew that someone had come out from behind the large tree in the square, and was following her furtively. She didn't turn around to see who was taking those light steps, led by her long shadow. The city was very small, but life is always accompanied by noise and she couldn't always hear the sound of the footsteps. She knew, however, that many people followed her, at times out of curiosity, and at times, malice. It was the girl with a baby on her back who was following her that day, walking in hurried steps and keeping a consistent distance between them. She knew that if she turned around, the girl would turn around immediately as well and bolt out of sight, so she didn't. Then she forgot that someone was following her, and that she was walking on a certain street

Evening approached as she roamed about the city, not realizing how cold it was. She spotted a little diner, from which a faint but warm electric light seeped out, and went inside, like someone traveling far away and suddenly hurrying because she realized it was getting dark. The glass door was fogged up, concealing the shabby, untidy interior; the stained paper menus on the wall called out to the hungry in a friendly way. When she smelled the soup and side dishes being prepared by the owner, a plump woman, in the small open kitchen, she sensed her old friend, though more frail than before, coming to pay another visit. When this pale-faced friend called sorrow visited her, an obscure mist of sorts spread across her face. But the mist never turned to tears. She didn't really know very much about this friend. Very long ago, she forgot about tears, along with words, and didn't even know what they were anymore.

Nibbling at the food the woman in the kitchen had brought her, she turned her gaze to the small, dusty television on a table in a corner. The fast-paced images on the screen, once so familiar to her, flashed by without catching her eye, until she saw some faces that looked familiar, as if she'd seen them once or twice, appear and disappear. The lips on these faces, which all looked alike, with similar waxen smiles and pronouncing messages as empty as foam, were moving busily. She recognized one face in particular, among the countless others.

For a very brief moment, she was almost confused. Momentarily, she thought that it was a video of herself playing, but then she realized whose face it was on the screen. She stared at the face, and the details surrounding the face and the body, as if at strange relics from a past era.

The hairstyle that Conch had taken great trouble to come up with, that had made her the most beautiful woman in the world at one time; the blue suit Conch had gotten from a renowned designer, on the condition that the mark of the designer be imprinted on the outside; her distinct makeup, with two stars around her eyes, and a gradation of purple shades on her eyelids, which Conch had hassled over with the makeup artist, for television jobs that Shark continued to bring in; postures and movements that would remind anyone who was watching of her; some of these were creations that had taken years of work by countless people around her.

To find the best hairstyle for her face and body, for instance, Conch experimented with more than thirty top hairstylists, and made many changes even afterward. And the blue suit, created by a carefully chosen designer for the underwater filming of her last commercial, had been designed through special research and development so that it would merge with the water and make it look as if she were dressed in waves of water as she descended into the sea; the most expensive silk, whose weight and texture had almost zero resistance, had been used to that end, and the results were seen as the product of a successful joint effort by chemical engineers and textile designers. Only her movements and expressions were her own, which neither Conch nor any expert could impose on her. And all designs adorning her were created to highlight her movements and expressions.

The woman on the screen, with her hair, her smile, and her clothes, who made the same gestures and movements she used to make, blinked at times, smiled at times, faced the camera, and shed a few teardrops to express sorrow, often making dramatic changes in her expression. The woman on the screen, who looked just like her, was playing Jini with every fiber of her body, and with a vocal sorrow that immediately diffused the frustration people had felt at her, who was voiceless. The body and the face and the mouth formed a trinity, excited to tell people, rashly and without fearing any mistake that an unlucky copy actress could make, about the misfortune that the death of her little sister, Jini, had brought upon the whole family. The woman on the screen forgot at times that she had dressed up as Jini. Yes, the woman's mouth formed the words, "my sister's death," so many times that they couldn't be mistaken.

She no longer had to pay careful attention to what she was watching. She had the whole picture now. Everything about the woman's appearance and movements betrayed an awkwardness that made her slip away from the object of imitation in a wrong, unintended direction, like a line drawn by an unskilled hand.

"Oh, Starfish!" She cried out in her heart the name she thought she'd forgotten. When the camera left the face on the screen to capture the audience, she found herself searching in vain for another face, and her own took on a look of sadness, infinitely transparent and profound. She whispered a few names in her heart, as if to practice the pronunciation of some basic vocabulary of a dead language.

'Agar-Agar, Shark, Starfish—Oh, and Conch.'

No one she knew had been among the audience at the studio. The screen was once again filled with images of Starfish.

The owner of the diner came out from the kitchen and sat down a table across from her, and began to eat a late dinner, her face fixed on the television screen just like her. When the owner, who'd been watching the screen, turned around in surprise, she, who'd been sitting there just now, had already disappeared into the dark street. Only a few shiny coins remained where she'd been.

Agar-Agar

"THAT SUMMER WE were all insane!" the woman wailed, heaving a great sigh, heavy with the weight of one atoning for her sins, a sigh rising from deep within the gut.

Her violent sigh extinguished the candle that was in a crevice of a rock. It was the dead of night. There was no moonlight, with the moon hidden behind the low clouds that covered the ridge and that looked as if they would start scattering snow any minute. The murky light that climbed up doggedly from the city seemed, to the woman, to foretell a darker world to come. There was no light around the woman, except for the candlelight in the vinyl tent pitched among some rocks below, where a group of people was praying. In the darkness, she shut her eyes tight. She was being tormented by the images that jumped out of her mind every night, which hovered hazily before her eyes at first, then suddenly became clear; the images that took her to the extremes, once they seized her. Her body was as hot as an oven because of the images, and she would get butterflies in her stomach all the time; her mouth spilled out profanities despite herself, to rid her mind of them.

She began to utter the names of all the gods she knew, waving her hands as if to chase away flying insects, as if shaking a talisman at the sinister images that were stirring in her mind, waiting for a chance to jump out. But she didn't have a very good memory, and she would end up staying all night, repeatedly calling out the names, which had never worked any miracle for her, in a haphazard order.

That night of darkness, however, was quite strange. The wind that night wasn't particularly strong, but when she lit the candle, the light would go out, and when she lit it again, the light would go out again in a moment. The results were the same when she straightened up the black candlewick, and when she turned her head aside and sighed in the direction opposite from the candle. The flame would go out and make the darkness around her even thicker. Several images, very vivid, flashed before her eyes in the darkness, bursting out of her mind like a tidal wave or volcanic eruption but without a sound of the explosion, stopping her animal-like wails.

She couldn't remember exactly how many years had passed. At times it felt as if what happened took place in a distant past, even a past life. But the more she ran from it, the more it lunged at her as if it happened yesterday. During that summer that always came alive to her again, as if it were yesterday, her youngest baby girl was just beginning to grow. Her skin was so delicate that it looked like the heart of a Chinese cabbage, which you wanted to take a bite of, and there was a pure beauty about the girl, even at that young age, that made people stop in their tracks. The birth had been easy, and she had felt unburdened, as if she'd set down a heavy load. And the child was no trouble, except that she was delicate and sickly. This little child, however, had a job. From early on, she went from studio to dusty studio, on shaky buses, and wherever else she was wanted, in order to feed her family, and she grew weaker and weaker. So all the little ailments in the world paid the woman a visit, and each time, her breasts became more worn out, and soon they were so flat that they barely showed at all. When she went out to the market with her disheveled hair, wearing loose pants, people often called her "Mister."

The woman had a clear view of the little house, as if she had just come out of it and turned around to look—the house they had managed to buy at the cost of the health of the little girl, who endured through illness big and small, the house whose cemented yard was decorated with a brick flowerbed where rose mosses grew. The door of the house was blue, with the paint peeling here and there, and her oldest and second oldest had called it the blue-door house. Her youngest called it by the same name, before she lost her voice. But did the girl really speak at one time? And how many years did they live in that house? She couldn't recall. She didn't remember such things, though she could plainly see things like the rusty nail that had been driven into the wrong place on the doorpost, and the cracks in the cement yard from which earthworms crawled out from time to time. For a long time, whenever she pictured the house, all she could do was stand there looking blank, mumbling, "Why didn't I ever pull out that nail hanging loose on the doorpost? Why didn't I get some cement and fill up those cracks in the yard?"

On this night, she clearly recalled one of the rooms in the house, a long, dark room where mold grew on the wallpaper that summer. The door of the room in her memory would open at any time, even if she didn't turn the doorknob, and come alive with smells and images. The incident that took place in a corner of this room, never disclosed, would replay in her mind erratically, taking on its own atmosphere, light, and shape in the darkness, as if under a spotlight. Each time, she would cup her mouth with her hands to keep herself from screaming and stand outside the room which was shrouded in darkness, a knot in her stomach. She climbed mountains with this knot in her stomach, and her prayers rose in intensity as she struggled against her memories.

Her older girl was at her mother's in the country that summer, so her youngest was alone in the room.

"None of us were in our right mind!" she screamed from time to time, shaking her head as if to wake up from a nightmare. But she kept being drawn to that room, as if into a swamp that pulled more persistently at you as time went on. She heard the faint sound of her youngest breathing, who'd fallen asleep before anyone else. She felt as if she could see the girl's slender white neck, even the light brown spot under her left ear, which could be seen from the side. But the images that come to life again are erased by the heavy breathing sound of two men, which filled her ears like a shriek that rings throughout a tunnel. It seemed that one of them squeezed, and the other tried to stop him. Darkness fell. The woman didn't see anything clearly. Except the dark red bruises on her daughter's neck. How many times had she heard the breathing sound? She remembered that there had been many hands in the darkness, that the frightening hands had squeezed the girl's delicate neck many times, as if in a fit. At times they squeezed with the firm objective of getting what they wanted in exchange for the girl's life, at times for the pleasure of abuse. That's what she thought. For the peculiar pleasure of stomping on something tender.

Her son, well into his teens, had a solid build and was fiercely defiant, and his mind raced with a madness that no one could stop. It was just inertia, like fruit that leaks juice when squeezed, that gave him the desire, growing strong with his maturation, to squash someone, or something. In that moment when he crossed the line, that something happened to be the girl's neck. The body of the youngest had always been a fruit for everyone else in the family to feed on.

What was the woman doing outside the door? The hands squeezing the girl's throat, again and again, were none other than her own, rough and stumpy. Because of her worn out breasts, she'd turned into someone formidable. She wanted to walk into the empty room and expose all these painful secrets and end this life of exploitation. If the girl disappeared from sight, the pain would stop. Unable to bear the agonizing times that may overcome her with even greater force, she squeezed the girl's delicately beautiful, remarkably long and white neck for reasons all her own.

How long had she been squeezing the girl's neck? For some time now, she'd been wandering far beyond the boundary, the boundary of the validity of her memory. In those moments, images upon images, which she tried not to see, flashed before her eyes. Sometimes the images were of the endless checkups and useless treatments at the hospital, where she'd taken the girl, accompanied by the girl's father who came back to life at times, and was dead at others. What's done is done, he'd said, blinking his eyes slowly, but then he'd thrown himself into making negotiations, sputtering and glaring; and brought a yellow envelope full of bills one day. Everyone knew that the money was for the wounds inflicted on the girl, for the voice she had lost; yet they all kept silent. Who had given him the money? And for what? But the woman's mind, full of countless people and broken memories, was too confined for these thoughts to grow. Her husband died, without even spending the money.

Afterward, the woman suffered from insomnia because of the heavy breathing sound she heard every night while she lived in the blue-door house. Everywhere in that house, she saw hands, with tendons standing out, squeezing a delicate neck. In that house, all the hands in the world squeezed her daughter's delicate neck again and again. Even after they moved, and even when she avoided the neighborhood, the blue-door house always stood firm in that place where she collapsed in frustration, where she suffocated with grief.

As her thoughts drifted in that direction, her sobs grew louder and louder, and she could no longer keep the sound inside her mouth. She leaped to her feet, like a soaring pillar of fire. Then she began to run down the dark mountainside, so vigorously that it looked like she was flying. How many times had she run down the mountain in this way, as if to put an end to the world?

Lionfish

IF NOT FOR the goal of finding the little goddess, my trip with Icarus, accompanied by Conch, wouldn't have lasted ten days. Not even ten days into the trip, I came to suspect that Conch's so-called intuition was nothing more than the whims of an unstable mind. I put up with her stubbornness, her arrogance, her fussiness, everything. We had clear, distinct roles in Icarus, and I had no complaints about that. I drove, and Conch pointed the direction. What's important on a long trip, however, is the map reader next to you; what was important on our trip was the guidance of Conch, who claimed that she knew my little goddess well.

But never once did she carry out her role as a guide in a satisfactory manner. I didn't mind driving along the coast. Not going into the sea, however, while driving so near to it was a sort of sin to me. She never understood why, when we stopped in a town or a city at her orders, I sought out divers and stayed one or two extra days. It was soon proven that my initial determination to guide Conch into the world under the sea was as useless as the foam on the sea. Far from being interested in water, Conch was afraid of it. As time went on, I began to think that the day that was so important to me, the day when my encounter with the little goddess had taken place, might be more a day of torment for Conch. She thought that that was the day the little goddess began to make preparations to leave. The fact that Conch and I had completely different memories about that day had considerable effect on our relationship, not too positive. When we hadn't known each other well, recalling the minute details of that day brought us closer together. But as time went on, I learned that her feelings were different from what she had shown me at the beginning.

The only person besides my family members I'd spent entire days with was Pink Anemone; and we spent only about three full days together. I must confess that from time to time I had to leave Conch in Icarus and go for some alone time someplace else, to find some breathing room. I told Conch, of course, that I had some urgent business to attend to. I could return to Icarus only after having my fill of solitude, walking around unfamiliar streets in the chill of winter. I was an incurable bachelor.

She's gotten used to it, but at first when I left her alone in Icarus for two or three days she became almost hysterical. What, was I her boyfriend or something? She would pry, as if I were going out to see another woman. If I lied and told her I'd gone winter diving, she would ask endless questions about the divers who went with me. But as everyone who dives knows, even if you did get a group of divers together in a strange city in the middle of winter, it's not because you know much about them that you go into the water together; neither do you partner with someone because you feel closer to them than to someone else. What brings strangers together as a team to go diving underwater is the sea itself. Under the sea, people you've never met before become your partner in life or death. In that sense, my little goddess, who has compelled me to go on this Icarus trip with Conch, whom I'd never met before, is like the sea to me. Conch, however, didn't understand this, nor did she try to.

Conch, of course, was under no obligation to share all my habits. But she had no right to interfere with them, either. The fact that her sleeping habits—I'm not sure if I should say this, but she's a noisy sleeper—as well as eating habits are completely opposite from mine wouldn't matter so much if she fulfilled her role as a guide, which was essential to our trip. But while failing to fulfill the role, she began to poke her nose into my business, half in jest and half in cynicism. As a result, my little goddess seemed to grow more and more distant from me a month into the trip, even while I had paid for most of the traveling expenses.

What I couldn't stand about this trip, actually, were the things Conch told me about my little goddess on our long journey, which more and more often turned into a night journey. At first, she told me only very little about the little goddess. I frankly acknowledge that Conch is better at describing the beauty of the little goddess than I am. But as time went on, I sensed that there was a fundamental difference between my little goddess and the Jini she described, and far from helping me see the little goddess more clearly, certain words she used to describe Jini tainted the image of Jini in my mind little by little. For instance, as if to foretell a time when Conch's memory would grow dim, or the purpose of the trip would become tainted for secondary reasons, Conch's words became more and more abstract—"To really understand Jini, you have to walk barefoot in the summer rain with her"—and mundane—"I never let Jini eat anything greasy or salty"—and stated only peripheral facts—"You couldn't even imagine how many people I met for Jini's last ad. You wouldn't know these top artists with their incredible talents, even if I told you their names, would you?" I was, of course, thirsty for even the abstract, the mundane, and the peripheral. As long as they were about my goddess.

Still, there was a limit to how much I could take of these stories, repeated day after day. Not only that, the focus of Conch's
stories gradually moved on from "Jini, who had been with
Conch," to "Conch, who had been with Jini." Drunk by her
own words, Conch talked about her happiness and misery, her
love, jealousy, and hate. And yet, I wasn't brave enough to interrupt her. For I was waiting for that exceptional moment when
Conch's voice, tone, or words would make my goddess, wavering
faintly in the sea, come alive and make my heart pound. Those
moments, however, grew more and more rare, compared with
the early stages of the trip.

I must admit that I was quite hard on Conch at times, with
my suspicions of her. These suspicions, though, weren't without
grounds. What I suspected was that she had come to enjoy the
trip in Icarus, having forgotten her purpose. The Conch I'd come
to know had a powerful intuition, and had a knack for reading
your mind. At the beginning of the trip, her intuition was at
work and once or twice in a city we arrived at, at her orders, I
felt my heart shiver, thinking, "I'll finally have the blessing of
seeing my little goddess up close!" But such luck did not come
my way. From the words of the people Conch met in one city
where we stayed, we could guess that the little goddess, who
Conch always called "my Jini," had stayed there for some time.
But that was all. She'd always say that Jini had already left, and
where she was now was even more unclear.

As time went on, I even thought Conch might be making a
fool of me. Harsh as this may sound, Conch had nothing to lose
on this trip. She paid for only a very small part of the expenses,
though not out of stinginess, and I was the one who was doing
all the extra work. Not only that, she never looked at the map
with care anymore, and it seemed clear that she was enjoying
the trip in Icarus, which continued from night to night for itself.

When dawn broke, she'd order me to stop Icarus wherever we were and immediately drop off to sleep. She'd then wake up late in the afternoon and rush off somewhere to satiate her hunger, then return when night fell. Needless to say, I had to wait for her, not budging from my spot.

One early morning, I'm sorry to say, while Conch was asleep as usual, I took her journal from her bag, which she always clung to, setting aside everything else, and sneaked a peek. There wasn't a single new fact about the little goddess I'd hoped to discover. The journal was full of nothing but the same old, self-absorbed stories, most of which I had heard three or four times, and which she told so that I wouldn't doze off while driving a dark road, and feverish descriptions of night journeys. The awkward sentences full of excessive emotions felt pitiful even to someone like me, who had no knack for writing of any kind. Conch was but one of the majority of people in the world, an ordinary kind of person whose spoken words were better than her written.

After I read her journal, I felt confirmed in my vague suspicion that Conch was prolonging the trip to her own ends. But just as I couldn't interrupt her when she was talking, neither could I make any kind of declaration putting a stop to the Icarus trip.

Part Four

But what brought me ecstasy, even pain, was the expression on the woman's face, which revealed itself clearly now and then.

The smile on the face of the woman, dancing with her eyes closed, which showed through subtly at moments, was what I had been searching for so desperately.

I had found my goddess at last!

She Sleeps in a Half-Moon Cave

SOMEONE MUST HAVE seen her climb down the mountain on a bright night, for the people of the village at the foot of the mountain, living scattered here and there, said that she climbed down to the fountain on a moonlit rope at night. It was true. On some quiet moonlit nights when everyone was asleep, she made her way down to the fountain and danced alone. No one who saw her moonlit body slide down gently from somewhere halfway up the mountain, which surrounded the city and from which the sea could be seen in the distance, could help but stop in their tracks. But it wasn't often that she came down from the mountain at night to stay by the fountain.

The night is equal everywhere, but where she was, the moon was exceptionally bright in the sky. That's why people thought of the moon when they saw her, after she arrived in the little city and they gradually came to know about her dance. And when they saw her climb the mountain encircling the city at a late hour when the day suddenly gave way to darkness, they looked at her again, wondering if she herself had turned into the moon, so radiant was she somehow. So people talked, and more and more people who were interested in her began to learn where she lived.

It wasn't just the girl with the baby on her back who wanted to learn about her life. Many people climbed the mountain after her. People who knew how to be responsible for their curiosity, people who were aware, though vaguely, what their curiosity consisted of, and people who had opened their eyes to the secret of her dance after they had lost everything, followed after her, brought together by their curiosity about the kind of life she lived, which led her to radiate such beauty. They weren't many in number, but their number increased with time, and although they looked like ordinary mountain climbers on the outside, some quietly recognized each other.

The mountain ridge she climbed was gentle, but about half-way up it became steep, and thick trees blocked the view. If you pushed your way through the trees on your left at that point, you came face to face with an enormous rock blocking the way, as if the path ended there. Beyond that was a large rock face, and standing before it you could see the sea in the distance. The sea was tranquil and blue during the day, but on moonlit nights, it raged in fury. People knew that she slept in a cave on the other side of the rock. No one knew when she began living there or how she had discovered the place, a deep recess on the other side of the smooth rock face where not a single blade of grass grew, a place that even those who had lived in the village for a long time hadn't known about.

She just happened to lie down, as if for a nap, after chancing upon the place one day. A half-moon shaped dent on the upper face of the rock, flanked by trees that sheltered her from wind and rain—she came to love the spot. She knew that the sea stretched out under the sky before her, and the sky far away in the distance and farther away in the distance, but she silently gazed at the sea that couldn't be seen in any other season than this, when trees could be described as straight lines and curves, and the view around her which didn't really interest her. And without even feeling the chill of midwinter, she made the place her dwelling.

Even those who followed her halfway up the mountain did not cross the boundary of the rock. No one, at least, was so rash as to go around the precarious rock face and trespass when they knew she was there. Besides, it wasn't so easy to get to the hide-out behind the rock face, whose existence wasn't known even to those who had lived in the village for a long time.

Following her, they were surprised by the most basic fact that she ate and smiled and slept, just as they did, and were even more surprised to find out, as time went on, that the fact that they could see her dance, just as she did around the fountain, whenever they wished, and that she slept peacefully somewhere in the mountain that surrounded the village, had become a natural part of their lives. People began to climb to the peak of the mountain where she lived, because when they looked at the mountain, something indescribable sank quietly down in their hearts, and they felt somehow optimistic that everything would turn out well.

Lionfish

DURING OUR STAY in the city of I, the relationship between Conch and me headed toward extremes. The city was only about an hour away, at most, from the lab where I used to work. I felt disheartened, as if I'd come back to the starting point without any results, and also had a vague feeling that the end of the trip was approaching even though its purpose hadn't been accomplished. Not only that, the thought that the further we went, the further away we were growing from any traces of the little goddess made me doubt the purpose of this trip with Conch altogether. One day, when it was unusually warm for winter, I roamed the main street of the little city, which took only an hour to look around, wondering about the possibility of going for a winter dive. Then I went into a restaurant, and there heard someone talk about a dancing woman she'd seen in a nearby city.

Her story was simple. There was a beggar woman who came to the city hall fountain every day and danced a strange dance. She was so beautiful that you forgot about her shabbiness; her dance had a strange power over you that made you stop in your tracks; and those who saw her dance became oblivious to time, as if dreaming. As I listened to the words of the young woman, who said she was determined to go see her when she didn't have to work, I felt a shiver. It was as if I was cold, or as if I was shak-

ing off the effects of alcohol. I'd never imagined the little goddess dancing, but from the feeling the young woman was trying
to convey, as well as her tone, I had immediately pictured the
little goddess.

Despite having imagined countless aspects of my little goddess, with the help of Conch, and seen numerous pictures of
her, which Conch kept with her and cherished, the little goddess
was always fixed in my mind as gently descending toward me
underwater. In the last moment, the image of the little goddess
vanishes, as if the distance between us is so far and absolute
that no matter how many times she comes toward me, I could
never meet her, or touch her. But as I listened to the young
woman speak, the little underwater goddess in my mind gently approached me and began to dance, her movements barely
noticeable. I felt as if I was alternating between high fever and
chills and sat down and waited for the spasm to pass. The trembling in my heart didn't stop.

I returned to Icarus immediately.

But when I returned, Conch was different. I hadn't said anything, but she was already putting her things in order in the
trunk of Icarus. Even when I told her what I'd heard in the
restaurant downtown, panting because I'd come rushing, she
did no more than listen quietly to my words. I suggested that we
leave for the city where this dancing woman was, but she neither
objected nor consented. She just followed me quietly into the
car. She sat staring ahead, with her bag on her lap, the way she
did for a while when we'd first set out. She was silent throughout
the drive to the city, and I didn't dare say a word to her. Conch
had already left, it seemed, before the trip came to an end.

I don't know why, but I parked Icarus far away from the city
square where the fountain was and suggested to Conch that
we walk to the fountain. Conch looked back again and again

at Icarus, which stood under several fir trees on the outskirts of the brightly lit small city. It was as if she was resolved not to see Icarus again. My heart sank for some reason when she didn't object to my suggestion to go see the dancing woman, as the woman might be my little goddess, showing a generosity of spirit uncharacteristic of her. What was she planning to do, and what kind of a surprise did she have in store for me? Like people getting ready to say goodbye, we arrived at the fountain in heavy silence. The crowd wasn't too big but still blocked the view, so Conch and I pushed our way through.

The moment I saw the face of the woman with thick, wavy hair, wearing a long dress of heavy gray wool that covered the ankles of her bare feet that had turned red with the cold, I felt a pain in my chest, as if my heart would swell and explode right then and there.

I had found my little goddess at last!

My pain, which was an amalgamation of all the difficulties I had endured and longing for her, was transformed instantly to ecstasy. Following the woman's movements with my eyes, forgetting Conch, the woman in front of me, and myself, I plunged into a fitful excitement that the movements stirred up in me. I can't say, in truth, that I found the image of the little goddess under the sea, which I saw for only a second, in the woman dancing before me. I can't say with certainty that the woman in the thin, transparent blue suit under the sea had something in common with the beggarly woman who was dancing in front of me. That's how vague and ambiguous the image of the little goddess was in my mind.

But who could say that this wasn't fate? Be still and watch the movements of the dancing woman. The little goddess lifts a hand and places it on her chest. Then she puts her hand on the top of her head. And then she stretches one hand up, and the other down in a curve, and bends herself in a diagonal line. The movements made up a rare language that no one in the world knew but me. It was the conversation Pink Anemone and I shared deep under the sea in secret, when we dove as partners. The dancing woman repeated the secretive movement several times, as if dancing for me alone.

But what brought me ecstasy, even pain, was the expression on the woman's face, which revealed itself clearly now and then. The smile on the face of the woman, dancing with her eyes closed, which showed through subtly at moments, was what I had been searching for so desperately. The smile on the face of the little goddess as she descended toward me under the sea. I felt myself relax, as if all the tension from my thirty years of life left me, before the expression that seemed to point to an unnamable state, something I might have to look for for the rest of my life. I felt that I'd collapse on the spot.

There was no question about it. I had found my goddess at last!

I looked for Conch, like a confused child who's lost his way. I wanted to tell her this truth I had confirmed, and ask for affirmation. But strangely, I couldn't say anything to her. Far from saying anything, all I could do was spread out my arms in her direction, trying to keep myself from collapsing. Her face pale and expressionless, Conch helped me stay on my feet as we made our way out through the crowd. And yet she didn't look away from the dancing woman. Despite the blank look on her face, tears streamed down her cheeks.

What on earth had happened? Seeing the little goddess, whom I'd so longed for, I had nearly passed out, with my heart pounding as if it would explode. Sitting back on a bench in the square, I looked at Conch like I was pleading for an answer. Still looking at the woman who was dancing in the distance, Conch shook her head slowly, looking calm but not wiping away her tears. Then she said, mostly to herself, I think, "Take a good look, Lionfish. That woman is not my Jini."

She took her eyes off the dancing woman for a moment and looked me in the eye, saying, "That woman is not my Jini. I know Jini well. So you must believe me. If you insist that she's your little goddess, Lionfish, then I think this is the end of our trip. I'll help you to Icarus, if you want."

Her voice was dry as she spoke, but the tears on her cheeks continued to fall, so much so that she couldn't go on speaking. I shook my head at her. I felt strengthened enough to start walking again on my own, as if her tears had rejuvenated my withered self. I extended my hand as she got up and was about to turn around and barely managed to say goodbye.

"I believe you, Conch. So we have nothing more to do together. We'll go our separate ways now. Good-bye."

Conch looked infinitely small and delicate as she walked across the square. Her trembling shoulders and unsteady gait told that she was sobbing intensely as she walked. Finally, she disappeared around a corner.

The woman was still dancing by the fountain. But some kind of a fear kept me from turning around and watching her again. Instead of returning to Icarus, I sat on a bench trying to understand the fear that had come over me as I waited for the dance to end and for the people to scatter away. At that moment, the image of the little goddess I'd encountered under the sea flashed vividly upon my mind and hovered for a moment over the woman who was dancing. Then the two images overlapped completely. I was no longer a lionfish with poisonous spines. I had become a different person.

Agar-Agar

HOW OFTEN HAD the woman run down the mountain, seized by the fever that coursed through her body, then climbed back up after calming herself? Every time she climbed down the mountain, she was overcome with extreme tension, because this time, at last, it might really happen. At any rate, she tried again and again to focus her mind. She turned around and gazed for a long time at the mountain engulfed in darkness. When will she be able to accomplish her life's goal without being subject to the flame? She had only just begun and had so much to shout out, standing on peaks of mountains all over the country, to her brothers and sisters around the world. And yet she might have to give up her dream forever because of the flame. No, she would have to, probably for a long time, if it really happened. If everything happened the way she'd seen in the flame. She examined herself, feeling reluctant, a part of her wanting to climb back up the mountain to raise her voice in endless prayers that sprang from her heart, bowing her head under the candlelight, under the moonlight. Another part of her desperately wished for the strength to finally do what she had to do so that she wouldn't be able to climb mountains for a while. It was always this way: two different selves would fight, and one would win in the end. She

waited for dawn to break at a bus stop that served as a shelter
from the wind, not feeling the cold as she mumbled to herself.
She felt anxious and bored, and her throat tickled with the desire
to utter a line of prayer.

She raised her voice, calling out the names of all the gods she
knew, but wasn't satisfied with its sound. She couldn't pray when
she wasn't on a mountain. How can you call it a prayer when you
didn't cry out at the top of your lungs, or pour out what's in your
heart? How can you share what's in your heart with the brothers
and sisters praying atop mountains around the world without
doing so? She scratched her neck once or twice, then gave up.

The light of dawn fell around her, eating away at the darkness. She saw a bus with its headlights on coming toward her in
the faint light in the distance. With a resolute look on her face,
she boarded that bus.

"Oh, nasty," she mumbled, putting the key in the keyhole.
She puttered about, not seeing the keyhole even though it was
midday because her eyes were weak. She fumbled around like
a thief sneaking into a house that gave off a bad vibe. She shiv-
ered, holding the cold key in her hand. She wasn't sure if it was
because of the chill, or because of something she sensed at the
tip of her fingers, which seemed to push her away. The house
greeted her coldly, like a husband lying with his back to you,
even though she'd been living there and taking care of it until
recently. It was a very good thing, actually, that she missed her
transfer stop several times, dozing off and on, and one of the
buses even broke down, making her arrive home rather late in
the day.

She looked stealthily around the house. Standing on the
wooden-floored living room with its unfamiliar arrangement
of furniture, she glanced at the thick weeds growing in the tiny

yard, and the twisted branches of the jujube tree that stayed bare through all seasons and had never borne much fruit, as far as she knew, then quickly looked away. Only her son's car, taking up half the abandoned yard, seemed vividly alive. She stared at it with greed, and again, looked quickly away. Then she began to look around the house again, taking her time.

She didn't have to go combing through the house. Her heart sank when she saw her youngest's valuables, clothes, and other belongings scattered everywhere; she had expected it, but she clicked her tongue and spat out a series of nasty remarks despite herself.

"Oh, damn you all! You can't put up with things even for that long, can you, you bloody little bastards?!"

Hurling abuses being her specialty, she shouted out in all directions to no one in particular.

A headless mannequin, standing stiffly in a corner of the living room, shook when she kicked it, then collapsed. Layers of clothing and accessories that had been draped over the manne-quin scattered onto the floor, and the hard, chalky mannequin, in its nakedness, received the abuses in silence. But only for a moment. The woman raised the mannequin back up, then picked up the arm that had fallen off the iron bar and put it back in its place. She always tried to control herself, believing that there was a close relation between the words she hurled out in her hoarse voice and the speech impediment of her youngest, who refused to make a sound. But no matter how she tried, she couldn't make the words rising up in her throat go back down. After going around the house, pouring out curses at every little thing that offended her eye and made her temper flare, she felt as if the house was more accepting of her. There was no one in the house—no Starfish, Conch, or Shark. Her son's room, which she took particular interest in, was locked as usual, and she tried to peep through the crack in the door with her bad eyes. She couldn't see anything, but the slight feeling that emanated from the keyhole was enough. She couldn't divulge it to anyone, but the dream she had on the bus told her that the time was ripe, that it could no longer be delayed.

Her hands moved busily and skillfully, in spite of herself. She picked up the scattered things and put them in their spots, scrubbed off the grime clinging to the floor, dusted off the furniture, and washed the dishes piled up in the sink with a clatter. Only then did she sink to the kitchen floor, stretch out her legs, and sob for a long, long time, shedding the tears that had seized her in the form of a red flame just before she'd come down the mountain.

Taking care not to leave traces of her tears, she opened the hood of the car. What was underneath always disturbed her, as if she were looking at someone's internal organs. At first, all the memories always got mixed up. But she knew very well about the internal organs hiding under the hood, just as well as someone who had worked for years at a car repair shop, or even better. For instance, Jang, whom she met on the last mountain she climbed, and was the owner of a popular car repair shop, and who joined a mountain prayer group after doing time in prison, was astonished at her knowledge of cars. She was the one who figured out, only after hearing a few words, the cause behind the failed scheme—a car accident suffered by his unfaithful wife and her lover—designed by Jang, nearly to perfection, which had placed him behind bars.

She had always committed her deeds with the knowledge she had picked up here and there over the years. Her knowledge of cars was quite substantial now after all those years of learning. She hadn't turned someone's internal organs inside out, but the internal organs of a car were quite simple, no matter how complicated they looked. She couldn't understand why she'd never once accomplished her goal, no matter what different methods she tried. But it was different this time. Although she didn't know all the complex names of a car's organs, she had talked to Jang about their shapes, functions, and locations in between prayers, and accumulated more knowledge. Without being overwhelmed, she found wires and parts, and turned, clipped, loosened, and emptied them with just the right touch, not too little, not too much. Then she closed the hood carefully. It helped a great deal that the black car was always polished to a shine so that no traces were left behind. Lastly, she loosened several lug nuts on the wheels, as if playing a joke.

Only then did she feel the flame that had seized her fizzle out little by little. She was afraid of the moment when her body became light, so light that she felt as if she would flop to the ground any minute. The regret that always came over her, that she had done something futile, came over her again, as well as the fear that her flame might be nothing more than what people saw as fitful rage. But peace always won in the end: the peace that came after she had done what had to be done, the peace that came after unloading the burden that had been weighing down on her. She didn't know how long this unstable peace, which made her feel light, would last. She picked up her backpack, almost crawling on her fours as if she'd turned into an animal. She closed the door, still crawling, then began to feel strength returning to her body in handfuls. As if evolving from a quadruped to a biped in an instant, she took her hands off the ground, straightened her back, got to her feet, and began to walk with her chest thrust out.

She climbed the mountain path with hurried steps. She didn't stop, even when she slipped on rocks and branches pricked her.

The countless people she'd met in her life danced in confusion inside her head, and she climbed up the mountain as if dancing, raising her voice to call out their names, dictated by something that surged upward in her throat. It was very strange. She couldn't help but shout out to her brothers and sisters praying on all the mountain peaks around the world as the words came flowing out of her throat, always bewildering her as if they'd come out the wrong hole, except for the curses.

"All whose hearts ache with love, all who are bruised with hate, all who set out on a lonely path at night, all who are brokenhearted and can't open their eyes in the morning, all who open their hearts, yet feel sorrow deep inside, all who leave only to return, all who return to life, no matter how many times they're beaten, broken, torn, and violated, all who feel empty no matter how they try to fill themselves, all who shout and shout yet have more to shout, all who pray on Taebaeksan there, on Everest there, on Jirisan there, on Kilimanjaro there, on the faraway mountain there, on the nearby mountain there, on the high mountain there, on the low mountain there, on the huge mountain there, on the round mountain there, on the square mountain there, in the Charyeongsan range there, on Hallasan there, on those big and small and high and low mountaintops there . . . ."

She Said I Love You

THE HAPPINESS THAT filled her was bright and transparent. It was deep and subtle, more of a state than an event, and suited her body which seemed to be in full blossom, yet would never wither, and seemed free of the order of time in which things fall and cease to exist. If anyone tried to describe it as a color, I would advise they give up. It was close to blue, but it was touched from time to time by a wave of something close to yellow, or pink. And at times, pure red described her better. Often, it was close to a neutral color. I should say it was beyond the realm of conventional sentiments that people ascribed to colors. It was closer to lines and melodies, and there were no indicators to point you in a direction. All attempts to discuss the source of her happiness, the true nature of it, are bound to fail, but that doesn't mean that you can stop trying.

As winter fog rose in the sea in the late afternoon, she lay on her side, listening to the music of the wind, before the distant sea and the circular pattern created by the nameless islands, showing faintly through the fog. The intensity and rhythm of the wind seemed to hint at an oncoming snow. She hoped for snow before she left the hideout that provided her with the most beautiful view. But she always had the most beautiful view, no matter where she was. So it didn't really matter. As always, the light of the day would soon fade away completely, and darkness would fill her eyes. She heard the sound of the footsteps of people going down the mountain.

She must have dozed off for a moment. When she opened her eyes, feeling fully rested, she saw someone standing in the fading light, looking down at her. A short girl, carrying a baby on her back and wrapped in a blanket that was bunched up like barnacles, came dimly into her view. How had the girl found the path leading to the rock face, which no one but she knew of? The path was dangerous and couldn't be taken unless you were empty handed and barefoot.

She smiled at the girl, a smile being the only present she could give, as she had given countless people, as she had given a young woman now with the name of Conch, so long ago that she couldn't even recall when, and as she had given to those to whom belonged the many hands that had squeezed her neck. The girl didn't have a smile to return. That's how it was. Out in the world, she met two kinds of people: those who returned her smile, and those who didn't.

She gradually awakened and could see the girl more clearly. The face of the girl, though it should have been flushed red after climbing the mountain carrying a load on her back, was pale, and a bitter smelling liquid came seeping out from her mouth as she flopped down next to her. Sure enough, the water bottle which had been hanging at her side at all times, like a weapon, was gone. The girl collapsed next to her, falling flat on her face. Only then did she realize what kind of risk the girl had taken to make her way to the hideout. She knew how a decision to stop existing brought unexpected courage.

You couldn't say that she had expected something like this to happen. But the moment she opened her eyes and saw the girl, she thought that she may no longer be able to see soft snow falling on the sea, or spring shimmer rising over the sea, or the sea roaring and turning over. A baby came wriggling out like a little caterpillar from the blanket that had come undone on the back of the girl who'd collapsed next to her. Without even whimpering, the baby followed the basic laws of survival and crawled into the cave with buttocks lifted, away from the cold wind. The movement was that of an adorably tiny lump of life. She understood at last what had happened to the girl, and why the girl had come to her.

She lifted the girl's upper body and laid it on her lap. Then she put her mouth over the girl's, and sucked the bitter and strong smelling liquid that the girl must have swallowed in order to find the strength to risk her life to come to the dancing woman. She put all her efforts into removing the liquid that hadn't yet entered the girl's body, in the manner of giving a kiss, the kind that the girl needed and probably had never gotten in her life. Soon, the girl's upper body heaved in convulsion, and she spat out the poison harming her body. The girl lay still, exhausted and unconscious. But with her ear to the girl's heart, she could hear a faint heartbeat. She listened to the soft, sweet drumbeat that came from far within the girl's body, with her eyes closed as if listening to beautiful music. If she let herself go, she might find herself on a meadow far away, from where the drumbeats came.

A whirlwind came blowing from down below and swept through the mountain where they were with a sharp whistling sound. She looked up from the girl and turned to the baby, who was screaming in tears as if to compete with the wind. The baby had crawled out of the cave to the edge of the rock face and was howling, looking down over the edge of the sheer drop over the blue surface below. The baby kept crying shrilly, then stopping, looking down at the raging blue water that was washing up the rock face, tangled in the whirlwind. When it stopped crying, the baby looked intent, as if trying to decide whether it should crawl forward or not, hesitating between the two sides of the boundary.

She moved her body, being dragged downward, and picked up the baby and placed it down on the young mother's chest. But the baby cried even more shrilly on top of its mother, who didn't stir. She sat kneeling before the baby. Still sitting, she performed what could be her last dance for the baby. The dance consisted of a few movements that were as light as dry leaves and as pleasant as play. She said to the baby,

"Don't cry, I love you so much."

As she danced, repeating the words over and over again, the baby stopped crying, exhausted, and covered the young mother's chest with its own small body. The baby, too, would hear the sound of drumbeats that came from far away, growing louder and louder.

She slowly returned to her spot and lay on her side. She picked up the cloth bag, soft from wear, which the girl had dropped on the ground, and used it as a pillow; she was now in her favorite position. Lying there like that, she clasped her hands and placed them gently on her chest. To no one in particular, probably to the countless people raising their voices in prayer on mountaintops around the world, and to a certain face she longed to see, the kind face of someone who had never looked her in the eye, as if she felt bad for her, or indebted to her, and who had hair like Agar-Agar that wouldn't stay down no matter how she combed it, and who only made gruff remarks, as if mad at herself, she mumbled the words she had spoken to the baby: "Don't cry, I love you so much." She earnestly repeated the words over and over again, until they grew quieter and quieter, then faded away in the nearly perfect silence.

The blue sea filled her view, whether her eyes were open or closed. Perhaps it would be better if it didn't snow this night. Perhaps she should dance to keep the snow from falling, so that the young mother and her baby could make their way down the mountain. Gradually, she forgot about the baby, the young mother, and the blue world that filled her mind.

Shark

I'M LEAVING FOR a barren island. The season is approaching when the upper hemisphere of the earth thaws, releasing heat and humidity. I hate this season, so full of life that it seems even everything that has died will come back to life, this season when grass and leaves grow frantically, filling up the world with thick greens, streaks of rain fall like bombs from a punctured sky, and gales come blowing from the vast sea. I'd wanted to start my life on an island in the chill and wind of midwinter, when everything is frozen all around. An unforeseen accident made me spend more time and money than I'd planned, and things were delayed until this season, but it doesn't really matter.

I don't plan on naming my island. I want to live out my life, leaving no traces, in a nameless place. I'm not going to show the island to anyone, or pass it on to anyone. If I can come up with a way to do as I wish, I will blow up the island. I'll vanish along with the island, of course. It wouldn't be bad to disintegrate midair like that, leaving no fragments behind, not even a single particle. But this is only the beginning. I have a lot of time to think things over.

You could say everything worked out in the end. I had to wait a very tedious, boring time for the insurance payout after I reported Jini's death. People in that line of work are fussy for no reason. But as everyone knows, there's only a difference of a few vowels and consonants between death and disappearance. Who on earth was going to deny that Jini had died? If anyone has proof more convincing than mine, I'd like to see them. Death does not always leave a dead body. It was an ordeal, having philosophical conversations with these people. But unless they found Jini, they had no choice but to pay me the amount they'd promised. In the end, it all worked out, and although it cost a bit extra to convince them, I'm not complaining.

If there's a kind of person not suited for a slowly corrupting, disgraceful death, Jini would definitely be one of them. I'm showing her respect and consideration for the last time by making her disappear at a point where everyone will remember her at her most beautiful. It suits my tastes perfectly, too. Oh, and Jini would agree with me, if she's alive somewhere. Even if she is, nothing changes. She won't be found, and even if she is found, there's no guarantee that I'll be alive when it happens. I've done what I came on earth to do. Reporting Jini's death was one of the final procedures. Life on the island is a sort of bonus.

I was almost unfortunate enough to die before I wrapped things up the way I wanted, before I put my plans to action. Oh, naïve Agar-Agar! Oh, cute little Agar-Agar! She most certainly deserves divine retribution. Did she really think she could make me disappear by tinkering with a few bells and whistles? Oh, tenacious Agar-Agar. Someone like me doesn't disappear that easily. It'll probably take my corpse as long as it takes plastic to decompose and disappear. I might even come back to life as a flourishing poisonous plant. That wouldn't be a bad way to come back to life. The plant would be called poisonous shark.

As a result of Agar-Agar's idiotic scheme, of course, I've sustained the biggest injury of my life. But having an injured arm and leg is nothing. I actually wanted them gone altogether. But the kind of capable doctors I loathe looked after my body with painstaking care, and succeeded in restoring it to the point where it wouldn't be too much for me to train my body for a couple of hours a day. It's not so bad to simplify. And you never know when science will advance to the point where one or two parts of your body can easily be regenerated. Not that I want to live until that point comes. I'm just saying.

I don't blame Agar-Agar. Her last attempt was a bit over the top, but it wasn't just that once that she tried to pull something like that. I do admit that I wasn't as observant or careful as usual, with all my attention focused on the island. But I was fortunate enough to react fast and jump out of the car. If I hadn't slowed down, that would've been the end of me. The more I thought about it, the angrier I got, but I made up my mind to be cool about it. Everything is a deal. I didn't sue Agar-Agar or report her to the police. Without a word, she gave up what she had to give up. So I could have the money, with which I could buy the island, all for myself. A pretty good deal, isn't it? I know that she would never abandon that habit of hers. And unless her schemes grow more expert and clever, there's no reason to make a fuss. I can put up with her, knowing that we all have different ways of enjoying ourselves. Besides, it's pretty exciting to live with the risk of being murdered by someone. It's kind of fun trying to predict what she's planning this time. Cute little Agar-Agar, my naive and stupid mom, who I can't put up with for even an hour.

Life on the island . . . will be like hell. With blue sea all around, and sharp rocks everywhere to step on. And nothing but the horizon in the distance. But I won't criticize the monotony of such a background. I'll be busy. I don't have a lot of time left. According to the calculations of people I trust, who I asked for an estimate, with my current financial status, I can spend about 913 days, including the day of my arrival, on the island.

I'm satisfied with that. I don't mind ending my life based on a condition that can't be shaken by external factors. There will be nothing growing on the island. Except for poisonous shark, which will be found only on the island after my death, maybe.

Don't get me wrong, though. What I really wanted was for the people in the world to leave their places. Everyone without exception, at once, immediately! And start from the beginning. But think about it. Is a miracle like that possible? Do humans have that kind of courage and dignity, I mean. So I, Shark, am leaving, instead of everyone else.

Okay, here I go. A hundred and forty, a hundred and sixty, A hundred and eighty, two hundred . . . . Good-bye, Earth.

Conch

IT WAS BRUTAL. I'd never imagined that it would take so long for me to recover from my shock. Jini, Lionfish, Icarus . . . Yes, our short trip was beautiful. All the quarrels we had, so petty, and so ridiculous that I can't even describe them all, and the conflicts between this man called Lionfish and myself have all become fond memories for me. How can I ever forget all the thrilling moments when we chased away sleep at night, talking endlessly about Jini, and bonded as one on our trip? The comfortable interior of Icarus, the music we listened to as it moved along, and the winter scenery passing by the window have also become fragments of memory that keep me alive. I should also mention that the peculiar smell filling up the interior of Icarus, and the profile of Lionfish as he sat staring ahead in the driver's seat, have become necessary components of my daily life, like air.

If I met Lionfish now, I think I could tell him why I denied that Jini was right there in front of me.

I don't remember exactly when on our trip, but I began to hear rumors of a dancing woman, which I'd desperately hoped Lionfish wouldn't get wind of. When I happened to hear from someone about the dancing woman, as Lionfish did, I began to fear that our trip would end in the way it did. What I feared even more, however, was the brutal ordeal it would be for me to see how Jini had changed. I'd become so weak that I didn't think I could withstand it. I neglected my role as a guide and became very undependable, more to delay that fearful moment than to prolong the trip. But the moment was bound to come, and in the end, I had no more ideas with which to misdirect Lionfish.

I didn't lie to Lionfish. Jini was no longer Jini. The dancing woman I met by the fountain that day, wearing a long, dark woolen dress like a lonesome priestess, with thick hair tumbling down over her shoulders, was no longer my Jini. Yes, my Jini, Jini who shared with me secret conversations, with an infinitely gentle touch that tickled my palm; Jini who smiled at me the first thing in the morning when she woke up; Jini who made me anticipate the sweet hour when I combed her hair to start the day, with her head against my heart that palpitated with love for her. The moment I saw the dancing woman from a distance, I knew that my Jini no longer existed in the world. Who can understand the pain that I felt when I confirmed that I'd lost my Jini, whom I had so longed for, forever.

I should mention that although she looked shabby and dark and was far away, Jini was more beautiful than ever, so beautiful that my heart ached. I understood at last why Lionfish had such difficulty every time he tried to describe the Jini he'd seen. And I had to acknowledge, with a humble heart, that Lionfish had perceived through a single encounter something that even I, who had so prided myself on knowing Jini well, hadn't seen.

The fountain sprayed light and transparent particles of water into the winter wind, and Jini, who was dancing barefoot with her eyes closed against that liquid backdrop, was no longer someone I could call by a name. Just as I had said to Lionfish, she was no longer my Jini. I'm certain that she saw me, and recognized me, when she stopped dancing with her eyes closed, and looked for a moment at the people surrounding her, with a smile on her face that had grown in depth and serenity, that distinct smile of hers, which I saw when I first met her, and pictured whenever I was having a hard time. How could I miss the faint shadow that came over the face of my lovely Jini, as if she felt sorry for me, when her deep, dark eyes met my face, contorted with pain? A shadow that seemed to say, "Oh, poor Conch!" I think it was at that moment that tears began to flow from my eyes. What had made me cry, therefore, was not the pain of losing Jini. It was the fact that Jini would remember me by that pitiful face of mine.

I didn't understand all this at once, of course. I thought I ran because it was too painful to face the loss of my Jini, to see Jini had gone off somewhere I couldn't reach even if I gave all of myself, and was shining even more radiantly without me. And I didn't know at the time that I ran from Lionfish as well. And that I'd begun to have feelings for him.

Sometimes I'm startled to find myself searching for someone who resembles Jini among the countless people who come to the advertising agency where I currently work. But how could I ever stop my search for her? If I ever find someone like her again, will I be able to once again abandon all that I have, and devote my greatest talent to her? I'm not sure. But that's not going to happen.

I once returned to the city where the fountain was. The air filling the empty square was clear, and the autumn sky, a cool blue, seemed to whisper to me that it was time for me to move on from the long, brutal days of parting and loss. Several seasons had passed since the woman who had danced by the square through the winter disappeared, people said. They told me that there was a tomb in the shape of the woman, radiating light, on the mountain where she had stayed. The tomb, in the form of a dancing woman, was the result of mountain climbers piling up little rocks one by one. Strangely enough, the pieces of rocks on that mountain absorbed light during the day and shone at night, lighting the path of those who climbed the mountain at night. Someone must have caught on to this trait in her, and come up with the idea of piling up the rocks in her shape. No one knows who had placed the first rock on the ground. But those who wanted to see her again gathered one by one to pile up the rocks, and as those passing by either removed or added a rock, the tomb changed in shape each day, each moment, as if dancing a slow dance alone. I, too, climbed the mountain, to see the tomb that radiated light and changed in shape as if alive.

The tomb stood in a flat clearing slightly above the rock dwelling where they said Jini stayed. It was on a spot where the sea could be seen, stretching out endlessly into the distance, and plants that liked dry, airy land grew all around. I took out about five or six small rocks from my pocket. The mottled, smooth pebbles were souvenirs from the photo shoot trips I had gone on with Jini. I placed the pebbles around the neck, to make the line smoother. Then I sat for a long, long time, leaning against a tree trunk facing the sea.

Did I wait for Lionfish to come up with a group of people, to see the tomb of the dancing woman he had called "my little goddess?" I don't know. At any rate, I never found Lionfish among those who came up occasionally but without ceasing, to caress the tomb or remove or add a rock. I was well aware, of course, that he had settled down in the city after parting with me, and was living a life that suited him best; that he was giving diving lessons and running a little shop that organized and supported diving trips, in this city with ideal climate and marine conditions for diving; and that on his off days, he climbed the mountain to build a tomb that most closely resembled his little goddess when she was alive.

I'm going to return to this city one day to see him, whenever that might be. Perhaps I'll climb the mountain at night, with a group of climbers including him, to see the radiating tomb. But I don't know yet when that day will be.

She Sat in the Wind for a Long, Long Time

THE WINTER WIND blows through again. It sways, strikes, pushes, and blasts, bringing with it the smell of the sea, then moves on to a higher place. Time passes through with unpredictable movements. Two months, maybe, or two seasons, or even two years. All wind moves according to its own music, a music written to be played only once. After a wind passes through, its music is extinguished. She lies on her side, listening to music. She lay down like that one clear day, and has been listening to the music of the wind and the waves ever since. Her hands are folded on her chest. If you listen carefully, you might hear her calling out softly to you. A message she asks the wind to convey, a light and cheerful whistle that somehow awakens the sadness that lies hidden in all hearts. Perhaps you will

She arrived here by chance one day and lay down as if for a little nap, on a spot at the top of a rock face, a half-moon-shaped recess with an entrance flanked by trees that kept bad weather at bay. And she came to love this spot, with the sky that was spread out before her, the sky far away, and the sky that was even farther away; the sea hid itself away when new buds began to sprout, when branches grew and became covered in leaves, and came to her only in scents and sounds then. Once in a while, a butterfly or two flew up to her and stayed. They would sit on the tip of her nose or the crown of her head, and fly around as if to comfort her, then disappear somewhere as if it suddenly occurred to them that they were lost. Leaves that had fallen and come blowing in the wind, then piled up through an entire season, filled up cupped nooks such as her armpits and curved waist, and lightly covered her face, neck, chest, and legs.

Her face is still . . . pale. One day, when the first snow came blowing down in sudden squalls and covered the area all around, she lay fixed there with a face so pale that it looked as if the moon had sprinkled powder on it. If anyone saw her, they would say that she breathed her last before the most beautiful scene in the world. A close look seemed to reveal the traces of tears, tears of profound joy that could result only from such a scene. But who on earth would see her? She was bound to turn to dust one day, the soil embracing her, a single leaf covering her, the sound of wind surrounding her, and the raindrops and snow-flakes becoming part of the sea she was looking at.

"Just a minute . . . right there . . . that light . . . up there . . . far . . . but near . . ."

Occasionally, people passed by where she was. Judging from their short breaths, there must have been a very steep trail there. But not everyone was fortunate enough to climb up so high. The wind swallowed the voices that passed beyond, panting and dying away.

Where was this place with light that was far away but seemed near, or was near but seemed far away? This place spoken of by the many voices rambling through. Everyone climbed up the hill, longing for light in the night, in the wind. The people passing by all climbed toward the light above, which seemed far away but was near. At one time, she, too, had climbed toward an unknown place above her. What and who was at that place? She, too, had once longed for it, like those who now climbed up the slope. Not anymore. Now, she longs for nothing. She has become part of this place.

There was no light there, actually. But strangely enough, when evening shadows fell, the rocks on the tomb began to shine in the moonlight. Even without the moonlight, they stored up the light of the day and spat it out through night.

The music of the wind became even more refined in winter. Spring or summer could never be a training period for the wind. No wind is the same as the wind that has passed before, or the wind that comes blowing after. Just like the sea. Wind that is changeless could have a name, but perhaps a consistent wind is no wind at all. Just as a steady current is not a current.

She lies here to have both the wind and the sea. They always move, and the movements are more unpredictable than any other movement in the world. How could hope be extinguished as long as such movements continued?

Gusts of dry wind came blowing in occasionally and hovered around her, as if to protect her from life's natural decay, scattered her hair, which had stopped growing and was spread out in abundance around her, tapped her here and there on her toughened body as if on a xylophone, and finally, helped her to move from a solid world to a fluid one, from a shape to an abstraction, from chromatic to achromatic, and at last to sink and soak deep into the world, not as a liquid, gas, or any other thing, but as something intangible.

CH'OE YUN was born in Seoul in 1953. She received a Master's degree in Korean Literature from Sogang University, after which she went to France and earned a doctorate in literature. She presently teaches French Literature at Sogang University. Ch'oe Yun made her literary debut in 1988 with the publication of her short story, "There a Petal Silently Falls." She has also translated many Korean novels into French.

JUNG YEWON is the translator of *One Hundred Shadows*, by Hwang Jung-eun. She is also the translator of *No One Writes Back* by Jang Eun-jin and one of the co-translators of *A Most Ambiguous Sunday and Other Stories* by Jung Young Moon, both published by Dalkey Archive as part of their Library of Korean Literature series.